I've Got to Write!
It's Like Fire Shut Up in My Bones!

I've Got to Write!
It's Like Fire Shut Up in My Bones!

Florence Levy
Darlene "Beckey" Fair
Doris W. Harvin
Norma McLauchlin
Suzetta Perkins
Nicole Smith

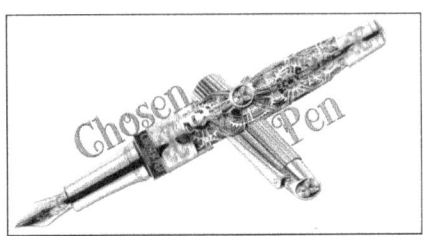

To order additional copies of this resource, write Chosen Pen Customer Service:

1420 Hoke Loop Road
Fayetteville, NC 28314
FAX orders to 910-868-3300
Phone orders to 910-818-6652
Website: www.chosenpen.com

I've Got to Write/ Norma McLauchlin
1.   Literary Collections–Fiction–African American
2.   Fiction-Spiritual and Religion
3.   Fiction-Inspirational
4.   Fiction-General
5.   Fiction-Anthologies
6.   Fiction-Short Stories

Library of Congress Control Number: 2019900727

ISBN-13: 978-1-7322366-2-2

Printed in the United States of America

10 9 8 7 6 5 4 3 2 1

This book is dedicated to every individual who realizes that they have God-given words smoldering inside, ready to be spread to those who are so desperately waiting.

What Others are Saying About *I've Got to Write!*

"These were very well-written 'God-given stories' that will keep your attention and leave you wanting more."—Arlena's Book Reviews

"Chosen Pen Writing Group did their 'thang!' This was a collection of anthologies with heartfelt stories of forgiveness, love, faith, and encouragement. Each author wrote from their heart and was transparent and vulnerable. I felt God's love, presence, and compassion while reading. These stories will truly minister to your heart and soul."
—Queenie's BookTalk and Reviews

"The stories in this anthology are all different, but they all have something in common; they ring true, authentic, and genuine, and keeps your interest."—Hope. Dreams. Life . . . Love Blog

Table of Contents

Introduction

The *I've Got to Write! It's Like Fire Shut Up in My Bones!* literary anthology is a diverse collection of stories that the authors have had smoldering inside over time. With the vision of Norma "First Lady" McLauchlin, president of Chosen Pen Publishing, and encouragement from such seasoned authors such as Jacqueline Thomas, Stacy Hawkins Adams, and Sharon Ewell Foster, this group decided it was time to ignite the fire and spread their God-given stories. Most importantly, Suzetta Perkins, the group's resident author, was the kindling for this literary work. In addition, co-editors Tarrah Jones and Dominique Lambright, editors extraordinaire, stroked the embers to bring this literary work to fruition.

I've Got to Write! It's Like Fire Shut Up in My Bones! includes works of fiction, creative nonfiction, poetry, and cross-genre pieces from members of the Chosen Pen Writers' Group. The collection includes literary works from award-winning writers Suzetta Perkins and Darlene "Becky" Fair; veteran writers Nicole Smith and Norma McLauchlin; and the emerging voices of Doris Harvin and Florence Levy. This anthology fills a gap for emerging authors who would not have had an opportunity to share their God-given words otherwise.

After reading these God-appointed stories, it is the authors' desire that readers are compelled to release the story that has been smoldering inside of them, waiting to be told. As before any of us were authors, we were readers first.

Each of us, including you the reader, has been called to write for such a time as this. God has people waiting for the healing that your words will give.

"You Don't Know Me"

Florence Levy

I am the One who knows hurt and feels the sorrow of the
pain that feels like no tomorrow.
You don't live in the shadow of darkness where gloom
knows your brilliant sunshine, yet anoints you every day.

You don't know that loss of pride, dignity, and shame all
lay under the covers at night ready to claim the rights of
your inheritance.

I cause raging wars and tear down walls; separating that
which may fall on you.
I bring on sharp, fiery thunderous storms of terror to
embrace your enemies.

To protect the ones I love, I watch over you.
With your swollen, blinded eyes, you can't see; you don't
know me.

I am the One who walks beside you, watching you trip and
fall, trembling as you get up. I rise quickly, waiting to catch
you in my wings, from the soft pillows in the clouds.

Holding your hands firmly and leading the way,
I anoint your head with fragrance, your cup overflows.

Day after day, I wait patiently for you to come home.

It's dreary and cold outside. "Come in," I will say. I will tenderly tuck you in.

Where has the time gone?
There is nothing new under the sun, I know, 'cause I am the One who is
I Am. Yet, you don't know me.

"Turn Around Surprise"
Darlene "Beckey" Fair

Chapter 1

Most times, the things you inherit include a house or money, but that was not the case for Lynn Hawkins. She stood five-feet and one inch tall, and was as thin as a rail with natural black hair that dangled to her shoulders. Her passion was designing and sewing women's attire, with hopes of someday becoming a top fashion designer. Lynn was the middle child of seven children, and was quite an energetic teenager.

Lynn remembered her great-grandmother Marlene and grandmother Marci talking about how they'd met so many different people, and how those people changed their lives somehow. She was a little skeptical, as she could not relate to what they were saying. It's not that she didn't believe them. Their stories were heartwarming. For example, they often talked about how everyone in the neighborhood was one big happy family. If one family was hurting, hungry, or in need, the entire neighborhood was hurting and in need, and did everything they could to help and support one another. Since her family didn't have very much, she didn't understand how what they had could be shared without leaving them in need as well.

Lynn's parents always instilled in her to treat everyone with respect, as had her grandmother Marci. *"Never burn the bridge you cross,"* her grandmother would say, *"you just might need to cross over it again."* Grandmother Marci was the glue that held the family together, and her words of wisdom were always valued.

On a warm Saturday morning, more precisely August 5, 1967, things began to unfold. It was Lynn's sweet sixteen birthday celebration, and she was quite excited. Even at the young age of sixteen, Lynn was determined to enjoy all that life offered. She lived in a small neighborhood in Central Florida where everyone looked out for each other. Families might not have had much, but they always shared what they could. On this day, though, it was going to be all about Lynn. Unfortunately, things wouldn't go as Lynn had intended.

After staying up late the night before, planning for her birthday celebration the next day, Lynn was in a deep, drug-like sleep when she was awakened by a loud noise coming from outside her bedroom window. She heard someone scream, *"Hurry up and get the water hose!"* Then the sound of a fire truck horn met her ears.

When she peeked out the bedroom window, the bright lights of the fire truck let her know it had arrived. She grabbed a t-shirt and shorts off the chair, got dressed, and hurried out of the bedroom.

Running from room to room, she looked for her family, but there was no one inside the house. She vaguely recalled one of her siblings calling out her name and telling her to come on, but she was so exhausted, she didn't take heed.

Lynn hurried toward the living room door to look outside. She froze when she stepped onto the porch. The Murphy's house next door was on fire!

"Come over here," yelled someone across the street.

Lynn ran across the street toward the crowd in disbelief. She was met by her family and neighbors from up and down the street. The Murphy's home was entirely engulfed in flames, and it appeared as though the entire neighborhood was helping put the fire out.

The Murphy family lost everything in that house fire, but thank God that no one was injured. Within hours, the neighbors were gathering things to help the Murphy family. There were all types of furniture and appliances being donated, including a kitchen stove and refrigerator. Food was also provided. Somehow, the neighbors had managed to gather clothes for all seven children and the adults in the correct sizes. One of the neighbors also offered one of his vacant rental properties so the family did not have to go one night without knowing they had the basic necessities of food, shelter, and clothes.

"Listen, children," Margie, Lynn's mother, said with a gentle voice. "We need to put together a few things for the Murphy family." Margie had gathered her family in the kitchen specifically to discuss how they could help their neighbors. "All of our neighbors are putting food boxes together, and I want each of you to pick out some clothes for the children."

The Hawkins had seven children, including Lynn's little cousin James, who lived with them. There were five children in the Murphy family. Both families had children around the same ages, and their sizes were almost the same. The neighbors always helped one another when it came to hardships of any kind, and this instance was no different. Instead of a celebration of her sixteenth birthday, Lynn joined with her neighbors to help the Murphy family in their time of need.

The Murphys ended up moving to another side of

town, but they continued to be considered a part of their old neighborhood. Lynn continued in her efforts to help in any way possible to make things better for the Murphys; they were like family to her. And little did she know at the time, but they would become more than 'like' family. They would become family indeed.

Chapter 2

One afternoon, a few years after the fire, Lynn was at the public library working on a college assignment when she heard someone whisper her name.

"Lynn! Lynn Hawkins!"

Lynn turned around to see Jason Murphy standing not far from her, smiling.

"Jason Murphy, is that really you?" Lynn asked with a silly grin.

"Oh, it's me alright," he said, looking at her with those bright, glossy, hazel eyes of his.

Jason was the oldest of the Murphy children. Lynn had always had a crush on him, but no one knew it. Not even Jason.

"Is it true that you joined the army?" she asked, already knowing the answer since her brother, C.J., who had stayed in touch with Jason, kept the family updated on Jason's whereabouts.

"Yes. I'm at Fort Bragg, North Carolina, and I'm on leave for a few weeks."

They chatted for some time before deciding Jason would visit Lynn's house to say hello to the family. It was not long before everyone in the neighborhood got word that Jason was in town and headed to the Hawkins' house to greet him. The entire community wanted to know all about his travels and future plans.

"Well, I do have something very special to inform you all about," Jason said with hesitation, "but I'll let you know at a later date." Jason left everyone in suspense as he shared last-minute hugs before saying his goodbyes.

Everyone enjoyed Jason's visit and was excited to know he was doing well. Lynn, in particular, had enjoyed spending time with her former crush before he headed back to Fort Bragg.

After Jason had left her house, Lynn went to her bedroom and fell across the bed. She looked toward the ceiling starry-eyed as she thought about Jason's visit. Lynn couldn't help but to allow her mind to wonder about what he had to tell them that was so special.

Deep inside, Lynn hoped that it wasn't a marriage announcement. "Nah," she told herself. If that were the case, the news would have already been spread across town. Perhaps he was getting promoted to a higher rank. Lynn couldn't be certain no matter what scenario her mind came up with. So, just like everyone else, she'd have to wait.

Chapter 3

"Does anyone know what's going on with that old market building on Persimmon Ave?" Lynn's father, Calvin, Sr., asked with concern. Mr. Calvin Hawkins, Sr. was a man to be admired in the neighborhood. He had a pleasant demeanor and the neighbors could trust him, as he'd proven his word to be bond.

"According to Mrs. Murphy, it might be a new department store of some kind," Margie said to her husband with enthusiasm.

Each day the old market building became a little more identifiable, but no one could tell truly what it was going to be.

The Central Florida weather was starting to get hotter than usual, but it did not stop people from sitting around watching the building be assembled. Each day was a big deal in their small town, and anything going or coming was noticed one way or the other. There were strangers in town working on the building, but its identity remained unknown.

One afternoon, there was a knock on Lynn's front door. Her youngest brother, Freddie, looked out the living room window. There was a tall, gray-haired mailman standing on the porch.

"Hi," Freddie said, looking up at the tall mailman upon opening the door.

"Good morning," the mailman replied. "I have a certified letter for—" He looked down at the envelope again and then back up at Freddie. "—Miss Lynn Hawkins to sign."

"Okay," Freddie said, before turning to call out his sister's name. "The mailman needs you to sign for a certified letter," yelled Freddie.

Lynn arrived at the doorstep, surprised to have received a certified letter in the mail. She hadn't ordered anything, nor had she entered any contests, so she wasn't sure what could possibly be being delivered to her that would require her signature

"Where do I sign?" Lynn asked the mailman, her nerves getting the best of her.

"Sign here, Miss Hawkins." The mailman pointed to a line on the clipboard he was holding. He then bid Lynn a good day after she signed for and accepted the package.

Lynn stared at the package momentarily.

"Open it," Freddie said with a demanding voice.

"No. I'm going to wait until Mom or Daddy get home from work." Lynn went from feeling eager to feeling anxious. "It's got to be serious, because I have never gotten anything certified." Lynn looked up from the package to her brother. "I have class assignments to finish anyway." With the package in hand, Lynn headed back into the kitchen, where she'd been working on her assignment prior to the mailman showing up on her doorstep. "Let me know when Mom or Dad get home. I'll be in the kitchen until then."

Freddie had a serious look on his face. "Come on, Lynn. Just open and read it. You can talk with Mama and Daddy later about whatever it is."

"No, Freddie I'm going to wait," Lynn said with finality. "And stop worrying me about opening this letter."

Hours passed before either of Lynn's parents returned home from work. Eventually, her mother was the first to arrive. Lynn greeted her mother at the door with a nervous look in her eyes, while waving the certified letter.

"What's wrong?" her mother asked. "Are you sick or something? What are you waving in front of me?" Concern laced her voice.

"It's a certified letter that came in the mail today for me," Lynn said. "And I wanted to wait until you or Daddy came home before opening it." Lynn looked down at the letter. "I've never received anything in the mail that required my signature. I hope it was alright that I signed for it." She looked to her mother for affirmation.

"It was alright," her mother replied. "I sense it might be something special." She smiled to ease Lynn's anxiety. "Since we usually share these types of special occasions as a family, do you want to wait for your father to come home before opening it?"

"Yes," Lynn said calmly.

"Alright," her mother said, then headed toward her bedroom. "Oh, by the way." She stopped in her tracks and turned to Lynn. "I talked with C.J. today, and he will be here for dinner tonight."

C.J., or Calvin Jr. as some called him, was the Hawkins' oldest child. He had his father's looks and a bit of his personality.

"That's great!" Lynn exclaimed.

Her mother turned back toward her room again. "And, Lynn, relax. Everyone will be home soon, and you'll have all the support you need to open the letter." She smiled at Lynn, which comforted her greatly and somewhat subdued the feeling of anxiety that resulted in not knowing what type of fate the envelope held inside.

Chapter 4

After dinner, everyone gathered in the living room and waited for Lynn to open the certified letter. The talk of the letter over dinner had everyone in complete anticipation as to what could be inside.

"Alright, Lynn, open your letter," her father said calmly.

Lynn looked around the room, then down at the certified envelope.

"Open it! Open it!" her siblings said almost in unison.

Lynn slowly opened the outer envelope and pulled out a letter with the words "Turn Around Surprise" written on it in bold letters. *What is a Turn Around Surprise?* Lynn thought. She read the letter aloud.

"Dear Miss Lynn Hawkins,

This might come as a surprise to you, but your caring spirit and support during my family's darkest days gave me the courage to live. I remember the date well; it was August 5th, 1967, and it was on your 16th birthday. I'm sure you were only expecting to blow out sixteen candles on a cake and not see hot flames coming from the house next door. But it happened. You were a trooper that day and so many days later. I still remember the words you spoke to me. 'Everything's not lost. You and your family are alive, and you have people that are here for all of you.'

Later that day, you gave me $26 along with a note."

Lynn stared up in thought as she recalled the words written in that note.

Dear Jason,

I know life is worth more than $26, but this is all I have to give you. You and your family will forever be in my prayers.

Your neighbor and friend,

Lynn Hawkins.

Lynn smiled, then continued reading the letter.

"I was 19 years old then, but between the fire and your compassionate words of hope, my spirit was awakened. You gave your all and supported my family any way you knew how.

"I remember my mother always telling me that you were the sweetest girl. You gave her money from time to time from what you earned sewing for other people. Well, a little birdie told me that you always wanted to establish your own business, and you will earn your business degree this fall. So, it is with great pleasure to inform you that the new building on Persimmon Avenue near town is for you. Yes, it is your very own building. You can name it what you like, and it comes mortgage free.

"I call this your 'Turn Around Surprise.' You turned my frown upside down and into a smile, and my life has been the better for it. I will see you on Saturday, August 5th to finalize everything, and to help celebrate your 21st birthday. Please call me if you have any questions. Hope you still have the telephone number I gave you.

Your Friend with Sincere Love,

Major Jason Murphy."

Lynn sat frozen. Everyone else in the room was in shock and a little teary-eyed. Lynn stared at the letter as if she'd seen a ghost. "Major Jason Murphy. Our Jason. Is this really happening? I have a place to start my own business and own the building?" Lynn asked in disbelief.

"That's what it sounds like, baby," her father said, removing the letter from Lynn's stiff fingers so that he could take a look at it.

Lynn stood to her feet. "Wow. Count it all joy. Praise God!" Lynn shouted and then jumped up and down with joy.

Everyone was so happy for her as they congratulated her. After a few moments, Lynn stopped in her tracks. "Wait one minute, who was that little birdie that told Jason?"

No one in the room spoke up.

Come on, who was it?" Lynn asked, looking around the room from person to person.

Finally, C.J. let out a sigh. "Okay, it was me," C.J. said, smiling. "Jason and I stayed in touch after he left for the army. Keeping up with the home front helped him not to be homesick over the years. He's always asked about you, and I realized he cared more about you than he let on." C.J. looked sincerely into his sister's eyes. "He truly cares for you, Lynn." C.J. hugged his sister.

"That's alright, C.J. You're my oldest brother and thanks for being in the loop of my life." Lynn smiled.

Hugs and laughter were all they needed to end the night. After putting on her pajamas and getting in bed, Lynn's heart was still pounding. It all felt like a dream, but Lynn's dreams were actually a reality.

Chapter 5

It was August 5, 1972, Lynn's 21st birthday. She was more excited this birthday than ever, and had been unable to stop smiling since she'd received the letter from Jason. She informed Jason that the family had not told anyone about her gift. What she didn't know was that Jason had something else up his sleeve. Her brother, C.J., knew all about it, but as before, was tight-lipped.

Lynn celebrated her 21st birthday with family and friends at a backyard cookout at her parents' home. Everyone pitched in and brought their favorite foods to share. That was more special than a birthday gift to Lynn. Her uncle William made his special homemade, hand-churned vanilla ice cream that guests kept coming back for. It was a great day of celebration and seeing old friends. Jason and most of his family arrived around noon with gifts and flowers for Lynn.

Everyone was enjoying the fine southern foods, games, conversation, dancing, and various styles of music. Mrs. Murphy made Lynn's favorite three-layer, red velvet birthday cake. It was always so delicious and an instant hit. Lynn's mother placed a number "21" candle on top of the cake, lit it, and called for Lynn to blow it out.

"Let's all come over to the table," Margie said. "Come on everybody. It's time for the birthday lady to blow out her candle and make a wish."

"Please. Please," Jason said. "Can we have a few minutes before Lynn blows out her candle? There is something I'd like to share."

"Yes, you can," Lynn's mother said while wondering what he was up to.

Lynn stood with a knowing look on her face. She was sure he was going to tell everyone about the building he had gifted her.

"C.J. and I have a confession to make," Jason said, looking at

C.J., smiling.

"What kind of confession?" someone asked in the crowd, laughing.

"Wait a minute. It's not that bad," Jason answered with a chuckle. "We have been busy checking out things in the community. This community was so good to my family and me when we lost everything in the fire years ago. I have not forgotten how people transported my siblings to school and gave us food and clothes. I thank everyone for making sure our parents stayed above water while having to start over."

"You're welcome," a couple voices called out.

"I know it was just as hard for your families to keep our family going, but you did it anyway." Jason continued, "I left home with high hopes to return one day and pay it forward. I invested a few dollars over the years, and it paid off. We have been in contact with the owners of the Miller's old house near town. It's a large house with a huge backyard. We want to turn it into a tutoring center, after-school care, summer reading program, food drop off—you name it." He threw his arms in the air and allowed them to fall to his side. We are in the final stages and should have a closing date soon. This is for the children that need extra help with learning in all levels of education, and families that might need help."

Everyone clapped their hands and shouted their praises.

"Volunteers are needed in every aspect of this project," Jason continued once all the cheers had calmed down. "We will need to make a few minor changes inside and out . . . painting, grounds maintenance, and other things. The main thing is that this will encourage our children to continue with their education and give back as they move on. That is what the community did for my family." He looked to C.J.

C.J. gave Jason the thumbs up.

"C.J. will be the project manager," Jason announced, "and we are hoping to hire a few people later on this year. Also, we are planning a contest to come up with a name for the program, but more on that later. I'm sorry for taking away from the birthday girl's day . . . *again*," Jason said with joy and excitement in his voice. "But this time, hopefully it was a welcomed interruption."

Lynn smiled and shrugged her shoulders. "How can my little candle top that?" Lynn gave both Jason and C.J. a hug. "Let me blow out this candle before it melts all over the cake." Lynn blew out the candle while everyone cheered.

"I guess it doesn't get any better than this," someone said.

"Well, I wouldn't be so sure of that," Lynn said, and then told everyone about the certified letter she'd received from Jason and the news about the building.

"The entire neighborhood just got a 'Turn Around Surprise' as well," Uncle William said cheerfully.

"I know my parents love me and my siblings dearly and never gave up on us," Jason said. "I learned that life lessons are sometimes hard, but you cannot let that stop you from succeeding."

"Amen," Margie said, raising her hand to the heavens.

"I was truly at a crossroads in my life," Jason said, "but no one knew it. I was nineteen years old with no hope. Between the house fire and Lynn's words that spoke deep within my soul, I realized it could have been worse.

That's when I decided to talk with an Army recruiter in town to change my direction. I stayed in contact with C.J. We always talked about doing something for the neighborhood. I have been blessed to meet great people during my career and listened to what they had to say, good or bad. One day, my commander and I were talking about budgeting money and investments. That's when I started budgeting and investing money, as I wanted to return home to give back. I was able to finish my education because the Army invested in me while I served my country. I have a few more years to serve, but I'll be coming home to volunteer as time permits." Jason looked around at the people who'd supported his family.

"And until then," Lynn's father said, "the neighborhood is going to hold it down for you. After all, that's what community is all about."

Chapter 6

Several years passed since Lynn's 21st birthday celebration, but the memories were still fresh in her mind. Retired Colonel Jason Murphy and Lynn have now been married for five years, and were the proud parents of three-year-old twin boys, Jason Jr. and Calvin.

There had never been a slow day around their home or community. Lynn's business was named "Lynn's Welcoming Boutique," and her little brother Freddie and his friend Deon won the contest to name the center. After a unanimous vote, the old Miller's house was renamed "The Motivation Center," as everyone needed a little motivation to keep going. The people in their central Florida neighborhood may not have had much, but they continued to invest to make a difference in each other's lives.

Lynn understood what her great-grandmother Marlene and grandmother Marci were talking about when they said that the people, they'd met during their lifetime had changed their lives somehow. *Life itself is somewhat of a 'Turn Around Surprise,'* Lynn thought as she headed to volunteer at The Motivation Center.

"Tying the Knot"
Doris Willis Harvin

Chapter 1
The Dreaded Trip

Tricia White dreaded the trip home to Charleston, South Carolina. So much so, she procrastinated for weeks booking her flight.

The elder women at Tricia's home church, especially Mrs. Harvey, would always ask when she was going to tie the knot. The old ladies made Tricia feel embarrassed about not being married, and pressured her to find a man and settle down. Truth be told, Tricia was satisfied being independent, earning her own money, and making her own decisions.

Mrs. Harvey, the Sunday School teacher at Saint Paul's African Methodist Episcopal Church, was seventy-years old, but looked like she was only fifty at most. Her skin was smooth and wrinkle-free. She always kept her hair in a beautiful, bouncy hairstyle, and loved showing off her long, lean legs by wearing high-heeled shoes.

Mrs. Harvey's lips were enhanced with candy-apple red lipstick, matching the polish on her manicured fingernails. She strutted around the church as if she was a queen. Mrs. Harvey was on her third husband; the other two had died. The story is that they worked themselves to death trying to maintain Mrs. Harvey's lifestyle.

Mrs. Harvey had no problem voicing her opinion about *anything*. She wouldn't stutter when saying to Tricia, "Young ladies your age ought to be married and planning a family."

This angered Tricia, but she didn't respond out of respect for Mrs. Harvey. Instead, Tricia allowed her anger to fester like an open sore, and wouldn't share her innermost secrets about men, relationships, or anything with anyone.

Tricia brushed her unhealthy thoughts aside and got into the taxi that waited outside her home. She then directed the driver to take her to Hartsfield-Jackson Atlanta Airport. As Tricia approached Terminal A-Gate 3, she heard an announcement informing passengers that Flight 368 to Charleston had a gate change. It would now be leaving from Terminal A-Gate 12. Feeling stressed and with increased adrenaline, Tricia raced through the airport. When she finally arrived at her gate, Tricia heard the airline agent calling for all passengers waiting to board Flight 368 leaving for Charleston, South Carolina.

Once seated on the airplane, Tricia breathed a sigh of relief, although it wouldn't have been so bad if she'd missed this flight. When Tricia left home after having visited for the Christmas holidays, she'd vowed not to return until she found the perfect man to marry.

Now, it was March, Women's Month, and her mom, Fannie, was being honored at the church on Sunday. Tricia couldn't dare miss this special occasion. She was pleased that her mom was being recognized for her dedicated service to the church. However, she wished she had a handsome, successful man to accompany her to church.

Tricia couldn't stop thinking about Mrs. Harvey. She

thought about the Sunday Mrs. Harvey approached her, telling her how she'd baked a cake for Tricia's younger brother and sister when they'd gotten married. "*I am not getting any younger, and neither are you,*" Mrs. Harvey had added. "*Don't you want a cake too? What are you waiting on?*"

Tricia wanted to tell Mrs. Harvey that she was only twenty-five years old and had other things she wanted to do before getting married. Anyway, it wasn't her fault that her siblings had jumped the broom so young.

Johnny, Tricia's baby brother, got married when his girlfriend of five years got pregnant during their sophomore year in college. Johnny and Harriet dropped out of college at the end of that year. Johnny joined the army, and they got married six months later. Johnny was now stationed in Germany with Harriet and Johnny Jr.

Tricia and her sister, Linda, were only a year apart. Linda met James Hunter, an airman stationed at Charleston Air Force Base, in their hometown. After meeting him, Linda had shared with Tricia how her new beau was the man of her dreams. Linda was only in the twelfth grade at the time. She didn't introduce him to the family until she graduated from high school, for fear they wouldn't approve since he was older; albeit only a year.

The young couple got engaged while Linda was in college, and after Linda graduated in May, they had a beautiful June wedding the following month. Linda's parents did not like their new son-in-law, James, at first, but they grew to love him and accept him as family.

Tricia was so deep in thought, she didn't realize she'd sat between two men who looked like professional linebackers. She tried to find a comfortable position, but with little success. She felt like peanut butter between two slices of bread. Both men looked at least six feet tall and probably weighed over two hundred pounds. They were both dressed in dark designer suits with a colorful shirt and tie. They were good-looking brothers—hunks!

The men took over both armrests on either side of Tricia, as well as their own leg space *and* Tricia's. Their broad shoulders took even more of her seat space. Tricia's eyes moved to the men's hands, looking for wedding bands. She was pleased when she saw only a Masonic ring on one of the man's fingers. Smiling, she thought, *If I could just take one of them home.* She'd seen movies on television where women had done just that; contracted a guy to be their pretend boyfriend just to keep family and friends off their back. Somehow, though, Tricia felt that was something that could only be pulled off in movies. And even in the movies it was rarely—if ever—successful.

Tricia felt boxed in her seat, and it annoyed her to no end. She decided neither man was her type. They were rude and inconsiderate, taking over her space as if they owned it. Neither man even did as much as greet her.

Two selfish men, Tricia thought. She needed to inform them that she'd purchased a ticket for space on the aircraft the same as they had. If she were to be tormented, she'd rather it be by Mrs. Harvey and the old ladies at church.

After being forced to sit erect in her seat, Tricia's mind raced back to home. She could hear Mrs. Maple, a retired schoolteacher, saying aloud after one church service Tricia had attended, *"Hi, Tricia, you set that date yet?"*

Before Tricia could even get the words "Not yet" out of her mouth, Mrs. Maple continued.

Every passerby stopped and stared. Now, with an audience, Mrs. Maple didn't stop there. *"And the clock is ticking."* She then tapped her watch.

As far as Tricia was concerned, Mrs. Maple acted as if finding Tricia a husband was her top priority. Why couldn't Mrs. Maple and everyone else simply accept that

Tricia was satisfied with her life the way it was? She was busy enough without having to find the time to cook and clean for a man, and have him tell her how to spend her hard-earned money.

The voice of the flight attendant came across the speaker and pulled Tricia out of her daydream.

"We are approaching the Charleston International Airport," the flight attendant informed the passengers. "Please return your seat to the upright position and make sure your seatbelt is securely fastened."

Tricia couldn't believe an hour and fifteen minutes had passed by already. When the airplane finally landed, to her surprise, one of the men she'd sat by on the flight spoke to her and asked if he could get her luggage down out of the overhead compartment. Tricia wanted to say, "No," but when she looked up and saw his alluring smile, she stuttered, "Y-yes, thank you."

"My name is Terry, by the way." He stood to get the luggage. He reached up to the cabin and got Tricia's carry-on. "I noticed your unusual bag when you boarded the plane."

Tricia reached to take her bag from his hand.

"I'm going to baggage claim," Terry said. "Please let me carry it for you." He gave Tricia a onceover. "A woman dressed as fine as you must travel with at least one checked bag."

Maybe she'd made a mistake about him. This man may have potential. Once off the plane, Tricia introduced herself to Terry. "My name is Patricia White, by the way, but my friends call me Tricia. Thank you so much for helping me with my luggage."

Tricia was feeling hopeful. She thought this could be the beginning of something great. As they approached baggage claim, a gorgeous woman wearing a tight, black mini dress with a deep "V" cut neck ran toward them.

"Terry! Terry!" she yelled, waving her hand in the air. When she reached Terry, she threw her arms around him and began to kiss him passionately.

Tricia was disappointed to see him return the affection. She stood and watched them in disbelief and disappointment. When the woman finally released Terry, he looked sheepishly at Tricia.

"I am sorry, Tricia. I didn't mean to be rude," Terry said. "Meet my fiancée, Clara Henderson. Clara, this is Tricia, a young lady I met on the plane. I was helping her with her luggage."

"My fiancé, such the gentleman." She blushed and then extended her hand toward Tricia. "We're getting married next weekend." She then grabbed Terry's arm. "Honey, we need to hurry. My parents are waiting for us at our favorite restaurant."

At that moment, Tricia's sister, Linda, walked up. Tricia was relieved her sister showed up when she did because the moment had become quite awkward. Tricia introduced her sister to the happy couple before taking her bag from Terry while thanking him for his help.

Linda saw Tricia's checked luggage with the identical print to her carry-on coming around on the conveyer belt. She grabbed it. "I'd recognize your unique luggage anywhere."

Tricia's luggage was green and blue with the words, BIOLOGY, ANIMALS, PLANTS, and WATER painted on both sides. Pictures of people, plants, and animals were depicted between the words. It looked like a jungle with a body of water in the middle. Linda's husband had it designed for Tricia in Korea. He knew how much she loved science.

The sisters exited the airport, and Tricia thanked

Linda for arriving on time.

"So, who was the happy couple you flew on the plane with?" Linda asked Tricia.

Tricia instantly felt embarrassed and the expression on her face revealed such.

"What's wrong?" Linda asked as they headed to the parking garage.

Tricia explained her experience on the flight and her interaction with Terry. She didn't leave out the fact that she made the mistake of thinking he could be interested in her simply because he'd been so gentlemanly, helping her with her luggage.

"How could I have been so blind?" Tricia asked. She wanted to cry.

"You don't want him anyway," Linda said to comfort her sister. "I can tell he's a player. If his fiancée hadn't shown up, believe me, he would have hit on you."

Tricia simply shrugged, her sister's words of encouragement clearly having no effect on her.

"Sis, you are a beautiful young lady."

"Well, I don't feel beautiful right now," Tricia said. What Tricia did feel, though, was unwanted. How stupid of her to think Terry, or any man for that matter, would want her. Looks like there would be no chiming wedding bells in her life anytime soon, or perhaps ever.

Chapter 2
Tricia's Confession

"Let's hurry. You remember our high school principal, Mr. Green?" Linda said as they reached her car. Without waiting for Tricia to respond she said, "His daughter, Elizabeth, is getting married at two o'clock at our church."

Okay, so Tricia was mistaken. There would be wedding bells in her life, but they wouldn't be her own.

"I heard it will be the fanciest wedding ever." Linda popped the trunk of her car. "Mom and Dad received an invitation. But you and I can park across the street and watch the wedding party and guests arrive."

Linda always had been infatuated with the whole wedding fairytale thing. That probably explained why she couldn't wait to exchange vows herself.

The last thing Tricia wanted to do, though, was watch a wedding party arrive at the church, but she didn't say a word. No need in ruining her sister's excitement.

They arrived at the church a few minutes later. Linda parked in the empty lot across from the church. They had the perfect view. "Look, Tricia." Linda pointed. "Mom and Dad are walking toward the church."

Both women admired their parents. "Mom looks beautiful in her lavender dress," Linda said. "And Dad doesn't look too bad himself in his black suit."

Tricia stared at her parents from across the street. "Yes, they look amazing."

"Look at them," Linda admired. "They haven't aged at all. I hope we have those same genes."

The girls looked on as their parents entered the church hand-in-hand.

"They've been married thirty years and still hold hands," Linda said. I wonder if James and I will still hold hands when we've been married that long," Linda wondered aloud.

Tricia and Linda sat and watched the guests arrive. The ladies wore lovely pastel-colored dresses. The men wore black suits or tuxedoes. Some drove up in shiny, black Cadillacs, the chrome on the car sparkling from the sunlight on the beautiful spring day. One couple drove up in a Porsche. Mr. Green's brother, who lived in Detroit, Michigan, drove a 1974 black Cadillac Eldorado two-door convertible.

"Here come four baby-blue limousines," yelled Linda while pointing.

The limos carried most of the wedding party. Tricia now seemed to be beyond excited. She'd participated in several weddings, but had never seen this much fanfare. The doors opened to one of the limos. Out stepped all the grandparents. The ladies were dressed in beautiful midi-length dresses with bolero jackets. Both men wore black tuxedoes and white shirts.

After the grandparents entered the church, the groom's parents stepped out of the next limo.

"I wish we could get closer without being seen," Linda said.

From their view, they could tell the mother was wearing a pastel-colored A-line gown with a short jacket. The dad wore a black tuxedo with a white shirt. The sisters watched the groom's parents disappear inside, the mother dabbing her eyes while being comforted by her husband's arm that was wrapped around her shoulders.

Another door opened, and three adorable children emerged. They looked to be four or five years old. The two little girls, with their candy curls bouncing, walked proudly, carefully smoothing their fancy white dresses with their hands to assure they looked perfect. The little boy tugged on the back of his tux and raised his hand, patting his bowtie to make sure it was still in place. He paused beside the limo, with his hands in his pockets, as he waited to be escorted inside the church by an adult. The children looked charming.

Beautiful young ladies dressed in pastel-blue formal gowns clustered around the children. They appeared excited, checking each other's dresses and hair, making sure everything was in place.

As they began to line up, the bride's mother appeared. It seemed as if time stood still when she sashayed to the front of the line in her gorgeous, name brand, ball gown.

"Wow!" Tricia said. "I see the bride. She looks like a fairy princess with her father on one side and her maid-of-honor walking behind them."

The bride's train stretched out on her stunning white wedding gown and shimmered like diamonds. The bride walked cautiously toward the church, clinging to her father's arm. Linda and Tricia were in absolute awe.

"Elizabeth looks happy." Tricia was completely mesmerized. She hadn't expected to get so caught up in the moment. She went from not wanting to see a wedding, to wishing it were her own wedding. "She's the most beautiful bride I've ever seen. I hope to marry one day." Those last words slipped out of Tricia's mouth before she even had the chance to catch them. She turned and looked at Linda, who was staring at her in shock, mouth wide open.

"What was that?" Linda asked. "Come again." She'd never heard her sister express her thoughts of marriage before.

Before Tricia knew it, words she'd never allowed to penetrate someone else's ears began to pour from her mouth. She confessed to her sister how hurt and embarrassed she felt when reminded that she was still single.

"That's the main reason I stopped coming home so often," Tricia said. "I'm happy with my life now, but I really would like to find that special someone."

Compassionately, Linda responded, "Don't let anyone pressure you into getting married, especially the old ladies at church. I knew they harassed you, but I didn't realize how much it bothered you. Your day will come, and you'll find Mr. Right." Linda continued jokingly, "Let's go find someplace to eat. You won't find anyone sitting here in this parking lot."

The sisters drove away laughing and chatting about what seemed to be an extravagant wedding. Tricia and Linda dined at a famous soul food restaurant patronized by single men seeking home cooked meals. Tricia sized up the men as they sat and ate.

"You can't judge a book by its cover," Linda said. "You need to open it up to find out what it's really about."

Tricia responded with a smile. "First, I need to find a cover I like."

Both sisters laughed and Linda ultimately agreed.

When Tricia and Linda returned to their parents' home later that evening, their mother gave them the scoop on the wedding.

"It looked like a wedding from Hollywood," their mother exclaimed. "The reception was exquisite too. A delicious meal was served at the beautifully decorated tables. We felt like celebrities."

Tricia and Linda enjoyed listening to their mother's recount of the day.

Later that evening, the ladies watched their favorite show, *Good Times*, before going to bed. Linda was still there, as she tended to stay with her parents when her husband was away.

Tricia laid in bed awake early Sunday morning, listening to the chirping of birds near her window. Anxiety had taken over her body. Her stomach was in knots as her mind raced with the thought, *Will someone embarrass me today in church?*

Tricia decided to roll out of bed and do something constructive. She showered and dressed, and then marched to the kitchen and began cooking a southern breakfast. Her mom and dad awakened to the aroma of bacon sizzling and coffee perking on the stove. It didn't take long for Linda to get a whiff either. They all joined Tricia in the kitchen and thanked her for her thoughtfulness.

"I didn't know you were a great chef," Linda said. "You know the way to a man's heart is through his stomach." She winked at her sister.

Tricia rolled her eyes and put her index finger to her lips, warning her sister to be quiet. She didn't want her parents asking any questions about whether she had a man in her life.

"Mom married soon after graduating from high school," Linda said. "Her dream was to marry Dad, her high school sweetheart, and start a family."

Of all the conversations to strike up, Tricia couldn't understand for the life of her why Linda would choose marriage. Nonetheless, she obliged.

"College was not an option for Mom in the 1950s," Tricia said to her sister. "But Linda, it's incomprehensible that in the year 1974, there are yet so many people who think women ought to marry at a young age. More women are graduating from college and wanting to start careers," explained Tricia.

"You're right." Linda nodded while biting into a piece of bacon. "Mom said it was important to her that her girls receive a college education."

After finishing breakfast, the family got ready for church. Arriving early, the White family sat together. Mrs. Harvey, the busybody, made the announcements. While looking among the congregation for visitors, she spotted Tricia.

"Miss Patricia White is here today," Mrs. Harvey announced. "We are delighted to have you." She looked to Tricia's left and then to her right. "I was hoping to see you sitting next to that special someone."

Tricia could feel the sweat forming on her face. She felt humiliated, but smiled and said, "No ma' am, there's no one special yet." She looked to Linda, who was sitting next to her. "Not that my sister here isn't special."

There was a light chuckle from members of the congregation.

Linda rubbed Tricia's arm gently, hoping to ease her pain.

The part of the service finally rolled around where Mrs. White was to be honored. Tricia quickly forgot the anger and embarrassment she'd been entertaining just moments ago and focused her attention on her mother receiving a beautiful plaque from the church. She watched church members presenting gifts, and listened to pleasant and humorous things said of her mother. Tricia noticed how happy her mother looked and decided seeing her mother this overjoyed had been worth all Tricia had to endure at church that day in order to witness it.

After eating dinner at church, Tricia rushed home, changed into her jeans and flat shoes, and threw the last bit of her personal items into her suitcase. "In and out . . . and nobody gets hurt," was what Tricia told herself whenever she visited home. Unfortunately, the latter part never played out, as somehow someone's words always managed to prick her heart.

Mr. White waited in the car to make sure Tricia arrived at the airport early. Once they reached the airport departure area, Tricia said her goodbyes, then disappeared inside the terminal.

Chapter 3
Tricia's Flight Back to Atlanta

Tricia checked in at the airport counter, went through security, and reached her boarding gate within twenty minutes after having arrived at the airport. She was making great time—her plane wasn't scheduled to leave for another forty-five minutes. Tricia used the time to finish her lesson plans for the week. Once they were completed, Tricia sat and wondered who would sit next to her. Would it be another handsome, rude brother? She decided she would speak up this time and claim her space if need be.

Tricia's thoughts were interrupted as the airline agent made an announcement. "Flight 3312 leaving for Hartsfield-Jackson in Atlanta, Georgia will be boarding in five minutes."

Tricia stood and stretched her legs. When her group was finally called to board, Tricia quickly got in line. She was anxious to see her seatmates. While standing in line, she was pleasantly surprised when she spotted Laura, one of her colleagues who worked with her in the science department.

"Well hello, Laura. What are you doing in Charleston?" Tricia asked.

"My parents bought me a ticket to join them for a few days of their vacation," Laura replied.

Laura was single, but dating. She'd been trying to get Tricia to meet one of her beau's friends for about a year, but Tricia wasn't interested.

Tricia shared the details of her weekend with Laura. She told her how fed up she was with the old ladies at church pressuring her to get married. Now that Tricia had opened up to Linda, heck, she could open up to anybody about her feelings relationship-wise. Actually, it felt good to talk about it instead of keeping it all bottled up inside.

Laura laughed. "I get the same pressure, even from my mother. My father tells her to leave me alone. *Let her live her own life,*" she imitated her father. "*One day you may push her in the arms of Satan's brother.*"

Both women laughed and continued talking as they boarded the aircraft. Laura and Tricia managed to find two open seats next to each other. They talked and laughed the entire flight. They couldn't believe they were about to land when they heard a voice telling them to fasten their seatbelts and position their seats and trays for landing.

Laura invited Tricia to dinner at a new seafood restaurant in Atlanta. Tricia declined at first, but Laura persuaded her to go. They agreed to meet at the Ocean View Seafood Restaurant after picking up their luggage.

Laura was from Savannah, Georgia. She suggested they order the big, hot-boiled pot, filled with a variety of seafood the locals called a "pot." She was familiar with all kinds of seafood. Her grandparents owned a seafood restaurant. Although Tricia's family lived in Charleston, she only ate fish and shrimp.

When the waiter returned with their pot, Laura gave Tricia a quick biology lesson on animals found in the ocean. The pot was full of crab legs, oysters, scallops, mussels, clams, and shrimp. There were also mini ears of corn and potatoes. Laura taught Tricia how to use a seafood cracker to crack the shell of the crabs. They dipped the crabmeat in garlic butter and delightfully indulged. Tricia ate the sweet, buttery scallops, but could not stomach the slimy, gooey oysters, or the mushy mussels.

It turned out to be an enjoyable evening. Tricia enjoyed her meal and her company. She and Laura sat and talked about their personal lives. Laura shared that John, her beau, was a lawyer at one of the big firms in Atlanta. They had been dating six months, and she loved the time they spent together. However, she wasn't sure if he was the one.

"Why are you wasting your time and his?" Tricia asked.

Laura looked thoughtfully at Tricia before she replied. "Neither of us are seriously looking for a marriage partner. It's nice having someone to share a meal, attend parties, go out to the movies, and have fun with. Why get married if we can do all of that without exchanging vows? Besides, how are you going to find 'Mr. Right' if you don't date? Who knows? We may fall in love. Right now, we are very close friends."

Tricia never thought of dating for companionship. She felt one should have strong feelings for the person. Then Tricia remembered Terry, the handsome man on the airplane. She had just met him and within seconds had fallen for him, and she didn't even know the man's last name! Perhaps it was because a man had never shown her that much attention.

"Laura, you are right," Tricia said. "I need to look for a friend first. Someone who shares my goals, values, and interests, then see what happens next."

"Well, John's friend, William, is still available." Laura made googly eyes at Tricia. "He's handsome, single, and a graduate of Fayetteville State College in Fayetteville, North Carolina. He is a professional photographer and teaches swimming at the YMCA. John met him at the 'Y' when he took swimming lessons."

Tricia thought about it, but not for too long; afraid she'd think herself right out of the opportunity. So, she decided she would go for it. She agreed to go on a double date with Laura and John that upcoming Saturday. Tricia had not dated much and was already feeling anxious about meeting William. She wondered if he would find her attractive or maybe think she was boring. Only time would tell.

Chapter 4
Tricia's Chance Encounter

It was Saturday, the day Tricia usually slept in; however, she had a busy morning ahead of her that included getting her hair done. Yawning, Tricia rotated her body to her left side and patted the pillow. She could stay in that position forever. Reaching for the clock on her dresser, Tricia turned it around to read the digital numbers that announced it was seven o'clock—time for her to get up.

Two more minutes, she thought, and then she'd get up.

Finally, she complied and pushed her body up from the bed to get her day started. Besides a hair appointment, she'd scheduled a manicure and pedicure. She wanted to look her best.

After a quick shower, Tricia went to her closet and removed her purple and black sheath dress. She always got compliments when she wore it. She matched it with a chunky purple necklace, large hoop earrings, and her black heels. Laura told her they were going to an upscale restaurant for dinner and maybe dancing afterward if the evening went well. Tricia decided to meet them at the restaurant in the event she wanted to leave early.

Tricia was pleased with all the pampering she had done. Her hair was clean; her manicure and pedicure made her feel like a brand-new woman. However, when Tricia returned home, she felt stressed. She called Linda and told her about her upcoming blind date. If anyone could, Linda would calm her fears.

Linda was delighted her sister was going on a date. Tricia didn't have much experience in dating, but Linda would be in her corner to guide her through.

"Be yourself. You are beautiful inside and out," Linda said. "My big sister is brilliant too. If he can't see how wonderful you are, there's something wrong with him. You get up from the table and run as fast as you can away from him."

Both sisters burst into laughter.

"Thank you, Sis," Tricia said. "You made me feel better. I'll let you know how the date goes."

Upon hanging up the phone, Tricia took a warm bubble bath. She was afraid the heat might sweat out her new hairdo if she got the water too hot. Picking up her washcloth, Tricia let the water ooze over her body until it felt soft and clean. Letting out a sigh, she hoisted herself out of the bathtub, dried off, and massaged her favorite lotion into her skin. Both she and the room smelled heavenly.

Now feeling calm and relaxed, Tricia finished dressing. She didn't want to be late, so she had to keep things moving.

Just before leaving home, Tricia put on her hot looking lipstick—the only makeup Tricia used. She didn't need anything else.

On her way to the restaurant, Tricia wondered how William looked. Was he as handsome as Laura had said? Was she taller than William? She imagined him having a muscular physique since he was a swim instructor. She would soon have her questions answered.

Tricia arrived at the restaurant ten minutes early. Just as she was about to go into the restaurant, she dropped her keys. A good-looking gentleman with a beautiful smile walked up behind her.

"I'll get that for you," he said.

Tricia smiled. "Thank you."

The gentleman opened the door to the restaurant for her, and she entered.

Tricia wanted to check her hair to make sure every

strand was in place before finding Laura, so, she stopped in the ladies' restroom. After making sure all was okay, Tricia made her way to the dining area where the hostess led the way to her table. She paused for a second; the handsome gentleman that had helped her earlier was sitting at the table with Laura and John. When she approached the table, the gentleman stood up to greet her.

"Tricia, this is William Watson. William, this is my friend, Tricia White," Laura introduced.

Tricia and William smiled and shook hands.

"You two are looking at each other as if you've met before," Laura said.

Tricia explained how she'd dropped her car keys and William picked them up for her, and how he'd also opened the door for her when she entered the restaurant.

"Ooh, chivalry! I like," Laura said.

Tricia blushed and then took her seat.

Once seated, William told Tricia how beautiful she looked. William was tall, dark, and debonair handsome. His smile hypnotized Tricia. She could not stop looking at him. Tricia wondered if his beautiful, luscious white teeth were real. They seemed to sparkle against his dark skin. He wore a grey and black sports jacket with black slacks. Tricia was almost speechless.

The waiter brought menus to the table. Tricia took her eyes off William long enough to choose her meal. They found out they liked the same foods. They both ordered ribeye steaks, asparagus, and baked potatoes loaded with butter, sour cream, and cheddar cheese.

Dinner went well. The two couples enjoyed their meals as well as each other's company. They sat, talked, and laughed . . . and, of course, ate.

"Would you guys like to follow Laura and me to the bar downtown?" John asked. "It has a dance floor and a

DJ on Saturday nights where we can exercise while having fun." He rubbed his full belly. "Work some of this food off."

William and Tricia both accepted the offer. William then offered to drive, and bring Tricia back to her car afterward.

In Tricia's mind, she still saw William as a stranger and was reluctant to agree to the arrangement.

Laura suggested that the group ride together. Everyone agreed to that arrangement. John and William walked out to get the car while the ladies went to the restroom.

"What do you think of William?" Laura asked.

"I'm attracted to him," Tricia said, "but I didn't feel comfortable riding with him tonight on our first date. I want to get to know him better."

"That's great," Laura said. "I knew you two would connect."

At the club, the couples danced, gliding across the floor, flapping their arms, moving with the rhythm of the music, while having a wonderful time. Everyone except Tricia drank alcohol. She had never drunk alcoholic beverages or smoked cigarettes. She always enjoyed dancing, though. Several times William offered her a drink, but each time she declined. This made her a little skeptical about William. Was he trying to get her tipsy? If so, for what? She managed to brush those thoughts out of her mind and enjoy his company anyway.

When the night was over and Tricia was back at her apartment, she reminisced about her evening. She would have loved nothing more than to go out with William again, and hoped he would call her soon.

The next day, William called and invited Tricia out to dinner and a movie. They set the date for the following

Wednesday. Tricia told him she could meet him for an early dinner, but Wednesday night was Bible Study. She went out on a limb and invited him to join her.

"Yes, that sounds great."

Tricia was shocked by his immediate response.

"I haven't been to church since my grandmother passed two years ago," William admitted. "So perhaps this is long overdue."

That Wednesday, Tricia and William met at a little soul food restaurant around five-thirty.

"This is where I get all of my home cooked meals." William chuckled. "I've never used my stove. After two years, it's still brand new. I hope to marry a special lady who will put it to use one day."

Tricia laughed. "Well, it won't be me. I hate cooking."

They both laughed so loud, other customers turned around to see what was going on. They quieted down and finished their meals.

"It's almost six-thirty," Tricia said after checking the time. "Bible study starts at seven, and it's about a twenty-minute drive."

William expressed how he wasn't ready to end the one-on-one time with Tricia. "I appreciate you spending this time with me. Usually, I find fault in my dates the first day. You have been perfect, despite the fact you can't cook."

Tricia informed William with a smile that she was, indeed, a great cook, taught by her mother. But slaving over the stove was not something she enjoyed doing. "Besides," Tricia added. "I'm single. Doing all of that work for one person is no fun."

"Hmm," William said. "Perhaps we'll have to change that."

Tricia blushed inside and out.

"I hope we can continue this relationship."

"I feel the same way, too," Tricia replied.

Tricia gave William the address for Saint James AME Church in case they were separated in traffic. When they arrived at the church, William teased Tricia about her speed.

"Were you trying to get me pulled over for speeding?" William joked. "Before riding with you, I will have to take a nerve pill."

Tricia gave him a playful shove. "I can't help it if you drive like my grandmother."

They laughed and went inside the church.

Reverend Wilson was about to begin the study. He was teaching from Acts 9. He started by giving a summary of Saul and how he persecuted God's people. "Today you will see that God can change anyone. He can choose anyone to do His work. You can be a teacher of God's Word, a thief, a murderer, poor or rich, married or single. Yes, and even a sinner. All of us are sinners." Then he continued telling the story of how Saul became blind on the road to Damascus.

Tricia was amazed at how interested William seemed to be in the class; asking great questions and making comments. He didn't sound like the new student at all. After the study, Tricia introduced William to Reverend Wilson.

"Please come back next week," Reverend Wilson said to William. "I think you would like to hear how God looked after His friend, Saul."

William smiled at Tricia and then replied to Reverend Wilson. "I would love to."

It was the beginning of what Tricia hoped would be a long relationship with William. Wednesday night Bible study became their standing date night. They ate dinner together at least three times a week, went dancing, and to the movies often. Tricia sometimes cooked meals for the two of them. William taught Tricia how to swim. He sometimes volunteered in Tricia's classroom, taking pictures of student's projects and tutoring problem students. William was a role model as well. With several invitations to parties and weddings, they became a couple.

After dating for three months, Tricia found herself always thinking about William. She hated the days she didn't see him. Tricia joined the YMCA to go swimming to be in his presence. She loved watching him in his swimming trunks, shirtless, stroking his muscular arms in the pool.

Tricia thought she might be falling in love with William, even though there was so much more to learn about him. Whenever she would ask him a question, William would flash his charming smile, rub Tricia's hand, and say that he'd rather talk about her. Tonight, Tricia was going to get answers, and William wasn't going to ignore her questions another day.

Commencing their date to the club for the evening, William knocked on Tricia's door, but went and waited by the car until she walked out. He wasn't the type of gentleman to blow his horn to signal his arrival.

He told her how beautiful she looked, as he opened the car door for her to climb inside.

Tricia kissed him on the cheek and slid across the seat, getting close to the driver's side. Once William was in the driver's seat, Tricia asked, "William, were you ever in a serious relationship?"

"Yes, I dated a young lady for a year. I planned to ask her to marry me. When I joined the army and served in Vietnam, she sent me a *Dear John* letter. She had found someone else. After that relationship failed, I was bitter and stayed away from women until I got out of the military."

Tricia nodded as she listened.

"I dated a few women, but you're the only one that stole my heart." William paused, then turned to face her. "I'm in love with you, Tricia," William announced.

Tricia was speechless. She did not expect to hear those words. She tried to move her lips to speak, but nothing happened.

Then she responded, "I'm sorry your relationship didn't work out."

William chuckled. "Don't be sorry. I'm glad it happened. I found you."

"I am glad you found me too," Tricia blurted out.

William reached over and held her hand. Tricia had more questions, but decided to wait until they arrived at the club. As soon as they arrived at the club, William went to the bar to order a drink. When he returned to the table, he asked Tricia to have a drink with him this one time, but she refused. He ordered a cola for her instead.

William took Tricia's hand in his. "Do your parents know about me?"

"No, only my sister. I wanted to wait until we got to know each other better."

"Know each other better? What else is there that you'd like to know about me?" asked William.

"Well, how long did you stay in the military? What did you do when you got out?" Tricia chuckled. "Heck, there's lots about you I'd like to know."

William informed Tricia that he'd served six heart-breaking years in the army fighting in the Vietnam War. His voice began to choke up. "I buried three of my best buddies, and I witnessed others injured. I feel blessed to be alive and healthy today." William took a deep breath and continued talking. "My last two years, I was stationed at Fort Bragg, North Carolina. My family lives in a small town nearby. I used my GI Bill to attend Fayetteville State College where I received a bachelor's degree in secondary education, with a major in history.

"I can teach history, but decided I didn't want to work. I get paid well doing what I like best, photography and swimming." He leaned in close to Tricia. "Are there any more questions, Miss FBI?"

Tricia blushed. Him being so close made her feel good. "Yes," said Tricia. As hard as it was, she stayed focused. "Have you told your parents about me?"

William laughed. "No," I wanted to wait and see if you felt the same way about me that I feel about you."

Their favorite slow jam filled the club. William took Tricia by the hand and walked her to the dance floor. William held Tricia in his arms as they moved slowly in a circular pattern, cheek to cheek, laughing and talking, with William occasionally stealing a kiss. The music stopped, but they were still moving on the dance floor.

William whispered in Tricia's ear. "I love you, Tricia. I never felt like this before, and I hate not being with you. I want you to be my wife. You make me happy. You bring out the best in me. I love you, girl."

Finally, Tricia realized the music had stopped, and then led William back to their table. Speechless, Tricia searched for words. She gazed into William's dazzling brown eyes. He looked so serious while waiting for a response. Finally, her lips moved. "I'm falling in love with you also."

William leaned over to kiss her, putting his muscular arm around her shoulders. Tricia felt safe and secure in William's arms. He then called for the waitress to order another drink. He pleaded with Tricia to have at least one cocktail with him to celebrate confessing their feelings for each other. She refused at first, but acquiesced so the waitress could leave their table.

Tricia asked softly, "William, you know I don't drink. Why do you insist on me drinking?"

"I'm sorry, Tricia. I feel like celebrating tonight. You didn't say you would marry me, but you did say you're falling in love with me. I only want us to celebrate together. I ordered a Pina Colada for you. There's not much alcohol in it," William assured her. "It's mostly pineapple juice."

"I'll try it for this occasion, but I am already overjoyed. I only need you to celebrate. You make me happy," whispered Tricia, "not alcohol."

Their favorite slow jam, "There's No Me Without You" by the Manhattans, filled the club.

Tricia and William had a memorable night. They joined in on the soul train line, sliding from side to side, moving their arms and hips trying to outdo the other dancers. They spent most of their night embraced, dancing to slow jams until the club closed. Afterward, William drove her home.

When they arrived at Tricia's house, William walked around to the passenger door and opened it for Tricia. "I know it's late, but may I come in? I think I had too much to drink. I need a cup or two of coffee."

It was late, but Tricia agreed. She invited William to have a seat in her living room while she went into the kitchen. When Tricia returned with the coffee, William was stretched out on her couch snoring. She shook William, but he didn't budge. "William. William, wake up." Tricia gave up, threw a blanket over him, and went to bed.

The next morning, William was nowhere to be

found. "William," Tricia called out, even checking the bathroom to see if he was in there, but he wasn't. It was clear he'd vacated her apartment.

"And he didn't even say good-bye," Tricia said disappointedly as she sat down on the couch, in the very spot William had once laid. That's when Tricia's eyes spotted a note on the table. She quickly snatched it up and read it.

Tricia,

Please forgive me for my behavior last night. I guess the love bug got the best of me. It won't happen again. Love you, girl.

William

Tricia was thankful William had left her apartment before she awoke. In being honest with herself, the thought that he'd had a hidden motive for staying overnight had crossed her mind. She felt elated to learn that wasn't the case. *Perhaps he is the perfect man for me*, Tricia thought.

Later that day, Tricia received flowers from William. She was in seventh heaven.

Months past and the relationship continued to blossom. Tricia decided it was time for her parents to meet William. Her sister had met him a month prior, when she'd came to Atlanta for a visit, and gave her approval.

There was a knock on Tricia's door. Tricia opened it and there stood William, looking sincere. She ushered him into the house.

"I'm in love with you, Tricia. You're all I think about, and I want to be with you every free minute, day and night. I want to love, provide, pamper, and protect you for the rest of your life." Then William took Tricia's hand, knelt, and tenderly asked, "Tricia, will you marry me? Please tell me you'll be my wife."

Tricia had to catch her breath before she could

speak, she was so excited. "I love you too, William," Tricia said. "I never dreamed I would find the perfect man who makes me so happy." She stared into William's eyes. "Yes, oh yes! I will marry you!" she exclaimed. No sooner than the words had fallen from her mouth, suddenly, Tricia's excitement seemed to dwindle a bit.

"Is something wrong?" William asked worriedly.

"I want to marry you, but . . ." Tricia's words trailed off as she bit her bottom lip.

William got a sick feeling in his stomach as he sucked in a breath of air, holding it until Tricia spoke her peace.

"But first I must tell my parents," she confessed. "Are . . . are you ready to meet my family?"

William exhaled. "Is that all?" He sounded relieved. "Of course, I'm ready to meet your parents!"

Tricia perked up again. "Then yes . . . absolutely yes. I'll marry you, William."

"Good." A smile stretched across Williams face as he slowly pulled out a stunning half-carat diamond ring from his pocket and slipped it on Tricia's finger.

"It's beautiful." Tricia stared at her ring with watery eyes. They embraced and kissed. "My dad is old-fashioned. You need to ask him for my hand in marriage. I don't want you two to start out on the wrong foot."

"I'm ready for us to start our life together as Mr. and Mrs. Watson. When can we go to Charleston?"

Admiring her ring, Tricia said, "I will call my parents and arrange for us to visit this weekend." Tricia immediately got on the phone and planned with her mom to bring home a male friend. "Now all we have to do is book our flight," Tricia said after ending the call.

William gazed at Tricia. "I will drive to Charleston. I've never been to that part of South Carolina. I'd like to see that huge oak tree people talk about and the famous iron gates."

Tricia responded with laughter. "Are you sure you are not trying to impress my dad with your Cadillac?"

"Whatever works." William gave a sly wink.

The week flew by, and Tricia and William were finally on the road to Charleston. They both were anxious about her parents' reaction to their news.

"What would you do if your dad says no?" William asked.

"He will say yes when he sees how much we love each other," Tricia said. "If that doesn't work, tell him you'll do anything to show your sincerity, even give him your Cadillac."

They both laughed hysterically.

William turned on their favorite eight-track, and they talked, sang, and moved to the music while cruising down the highway. The happy couple enjoyed the trip so much that they decided they would plan another road trip soon.

As they neared Tricia's parents' home, while admiring her engagement ring, Tricia remembered that William had not asked her father for her hand in marriage. After all, that was the purpose of the trip, so that he could do so. The last thing Tricia wanted to do was show disrespect toward her parents. So, she gently removed the ring from her finger and placed it in her purse.

When Tricia and William arrived at her parents' house, she introduced him to her parents as someone special that she'd been dating for months. William hugged Mrs. White and shook Mr. White's hand. Tricia's mom had prepared a delicious meal that included macaroni and cheese, collards, and fried chicken, and insisted they eat before the food got cold.

William smiled. "The delightful smell of your kitchen brings back memories of my grandmother's meals. She loved cooking soul food."

Mrs. White smiled also. "I hope you enjoy your meal."

Mr. White blessed the food, and the family ate up. Tricia's parents had used dinnertime to find out more about William.

William placed his fork on his empty plate. "Thank you for that tasty meal. I truly enjoyed it, as well as the company and conversation." He smiled and then turned to Mr. White. "May I talk to you privately, sir?"

Mr. White looked at William and pointed toward the living room. "What's on your mind?"

Both men got up from the table and headed toward the living room.

William talked as he and Mr. White walked. "We've just met, sir, but I've been dating your daughter for over six months. I wish I'd been able to meet you sooner. However, Tricia wanted to make sure our relationship was going to last."

Once in the living room, Mr. White sat in his favorite chair while William took a seat on the couch.

"I am in love with your daughter," William continued, "and I want to ask you for her hand in marriage."

Mr. White, with wrinkles in his forehead, sat for a few seconds staring at William. "Son, how does Tricia feel about marrying you?"

William shifted where he sat as if slightly uncomfortable. "We've talked about it, and if you approve, her answer would be yes."

Mr. White nodded his head and then paused. "My daughter is extraordinary, you know. I want her to be happy. I don't know anything about you or your people, so I will have to trust Tricia's judgment. If you are whom she wants to marry, then you have my blessing."

A smile spread across William's face.

"I ask you not to hurt my child in any way," Mr. White said.

William stood and assured Mr. White that he loved his daughter and would never do anything to harm her. He walked over and sealed his commitment to Mr. White with a handshake.

Mr. White called his wife and Tricia into the room. He informed Mrs. White that William and Tricia wanted to get married, and he'd approved.

"Congratulations," Mrs. White said. She hugged William and then Tricia. "When is the wedding?"

"We thought we would get married in November. I would like to get married here at our church," Tricia said.

Tricia and William were relieved that the cat was out the bag. Tricia was so excited and couldn't wait to show off her ring. Tricia never dreamed she could be so happy.

Sunday morning, Tricia and William ate breakfast with her parents. Before leaving Charleston, they visited the Angel Oak Tree and some of the famous Iron Gates. On their journey back home, Tricia and William discussed their wedding guest list and decided they would invite one hundred and twenty-five guests. William only utilized about twenty of the guests. He shared with Tricia that his family didn't communicate or socialize together for joyous occasions—only funerals, which always ended in chaos. He rattled off the names of several friends, but didn't think they would make the trip to Charleston.

"When will I get to meet your family?" Tricia asked.

William reminded her that his grandmother raised him, and she'd passed away. He said his family was dysfunctional. They argued and sometimes fought, which was why he stayed away from them.

"William," Tricia said, "they are still your family, and I intend to meet them." Tricia continued. "After all, they will be the grandparents, uncles, and aunts of our children one day."

"I'm trying to protect you, Tricia," William countered. "My family is mean and vindictive. They are pleasant only when they want something from you," William said heatedly.

The sound in his voice alerted Tricia that William was irritated. She looked carefully at his face and observed a frown.

Tricia ended the conversation, but not her quest for meeting the Watson family.

Chapter 5
The Incredible Bombshell

The weeks went by quickly. Tricia sent out invitations, ordered the cake and food from the caterer, and flowers from a local florist. Her sister and the bridesmaids agreed to decorate the fellowship hall. Tricia felt stress-free. Her dream wedding was falling into place seamlessly.

A week before the wedding, Tricia's mom received a disturbing phone call.

"I am William's ex-wife," the woman on the other end of the receiver stated. "He and I have two children together. Someone will find your daughter's body one day if she doesn't leave my man alone and call off the wedding." The woman hung up the phone. Mrs. White was horrified and immediately called Tricia.

Tricia's heart raced as she listened to her mother's voice quivering over the phone. "Mom, what's wrong?"

"Everything is wrong. Why didn't you tell us that William was married once before and has two children?"

Tricia was puzzled. She felt like she was on a speeding rollercoaster. "What are you talking about, Mom? William has never been married before and doesn't have any children."

Mrs. White relayed everything the woman had said to her on the phone call.

"That's not true," Tricia said, immediately coming to William's defense. "Someone is playing a horrible joke on us."

"Well, you need to talk to William right away. That girl sounded like a scorned woman out for revenge. We can't have a wedding with a threat like that," said Mrs. White, her voice trembling.

"Mom, calm down. I need to hang up the phone and

call William. Everything will be all right," Tricia said, trying to sound confident.

Tricia's heart was pounding as if she had just run a three-mile race in the Olympics. After ending the call with her mother, she dialed William's number and waited for him to answer the phone. She felt dizzy and had to sit.

"Hi, babe," William said. "How can I help my beautiful soon-to-be wife?"

"You can start by explaining why a woman called my mother's house claiming to be your ex-wife and the mother of your two children," Tricia responded sarcastically.

There was complete silence as if William had muted the phone.

"Hello," Tricia said, double-checking that William was still on the line.

William finally spoke. "I'm leaving work now to come and talk to you in person."

Tricia hung up the phone without uttering a word. Tears flowed down her cheeks. Within seconds, she let out a distressing cry. She couldn't accept that this embarrassing ordeal was happening to her. She hoped that when William walked through her door, he'd pinch her and wake her up from the awful nightmare she'd found herself in.

Twenty-minutes later, Tricia heard her doorbell ring, but couldn't move. She sat perfectly still, as her body wouldn't budge. She'd sat there allowing her mind to work up all sorts of stories, to the point she was afraid of what William might say.

William banged on her front door, sounding desperate. "Tricia, please let me in so I can answer your question. I'm pleading, give me a chance to explain, babe."

Tricia finally was able to pull herself to her feet and

walk to the door. Her eyes were red and swollen from crying. When Tricia opened the door, William tried to embrace her, but Tricia pushed his arms away. "I want to hear the truth." Tricia closed the door behind them and stood there waiting for answers.

"I'm sorry, Tricia," William said regretfully. "I didn't mean to hurt you or your family. Yes, I was married and have two children. I didn't want to take a chance on losing you. You're the most precious person in my life."

He explained how his ex-wife was a troublemaker, and he should've told Tricia about her, but his ex would have harassed her, just like she was doing now. According to William, his ex-wife was the same woman he'd planned to marry.

"The whole thing about her giving me the letter did happen. Only she wasn't my girlfriend, though, she was my wife," William confessed. "That part that I left out was that with the letter, I received divorce papers as well."

"And you honestly thought I'd never find out about this?" Tricia asked, dumbfounded.

"I thought maybe we could leave Atlanta after we were married before you found out," William replied. "I would have told you about my children . . . eventually."

Tricia began to sob uncontrollably. "Leave," she managed to say. "Just leave."

Once again, William tried to touch Tricia, but she pulled away. "I'm not leaving until you tell me that you forgive me. I made a big mistake, Tricia, but I need your forgiveness," William pleaded. "Remember Reverend Wilson said we all make mistakes. Please forgive me like Jesus forgave Paul. I see how much I hurt you and I'm so sorry."

Tricia walked toward her bedroom, still sobbing hysterically. "What do I tell my mother?" she yelled before slamming her bedroom door behind her.

When Tricia heard the front door close, she came out of her bedroom. "What am I going to do?" she asked herself, shaking her head. "I can always call the wedding off and try to get my money back for everything." Tricia went and sat on the couch.

Tricia remembered her wedding dress had just been altered last week. She wouldn't be able to return that and get her money back. The bridesmaids, her mom, dad, and sister had already purchased clothing for her wedding. The more Tricia thought about her circumstances, the more depressed she became.

Daylight turned into darkness and Tricia still sat on her sofa searching her mind for answers. Her phone rang practically off the hook. She refused to answer it. Her mother was expecting her to call, but Tricia couldn't find the words to tell her mother William had lied; that everything that woman had said was true. Tricia felt lonely and wanted to talk to someone, but was ashamed of anyone knowing how naïve she had been when it came to William, and believing he was Mr. Right.

Tricia did the only thing she knew to do. She began to pray. Tricia called out to the Lord to give her strength, wisdom, and peace of mind.

Later that night, Tricia found the strength to call her mom. "Hello, Mom. I should've called sooner, but didn't know what to say," Tricia stated. "You were right about William. I don't want to talk about it tonight, though. But I'll call you tomorrow. I need to sleep."

"I was concerned, Tricia," Mrs. White said, not quite ready to let Tricia end the call. "I didn't know what was going on . . . if something awful had happened to you. You didn't answer your phone."

"I know, Mom, but—"

"We must call off the wedding," Mrs. White stated quite directly.

"Mom, please don't do anything until I talk to you. I will call you tomorrow. I promise," Tricia said, and then ended the call.

Tricia felt numb, as if all her energy had been zapped from her body. As she laid on the sofa, she didn't want to think or move.

The next morning, Tricia woke up well rested, surprised that sleep had overtaken her. She thanked God for a restful night, free from thinking about her dilemma. She wished her life would revert to happier days.

Tricia called the school and asked for a substitute teacher. She told her principal that she was not feeling well. She wanted to share how her heart ached and how her mind raced; however, she was reluctant to talk to anyone, especially William.

Chapter 6
The Private Wedding

Tricia dialed William's number. "We need to talk," she said when he answered. "We need to make a decision on how we can tell our family and friends our wedding is off. How quickly can you get here?"

"I'll be there in an hour," William responded. "Tricia. I love—"

Tricia had hung up the phone before William could even finish his sentence.

Tricia dragged herself to the bathroom and looked in the mirror. "Ugh," she moaned at the reflection looking back at her. Even if she no longer planned to marry the man, Tricia didn't want William to see her looking like she felt. She showered and dressed as if she was going to work without a care in the world.

When Tricia heard the knock on her door, her heart began to pound. Tears started to flow again as she remembered her and William's last conversation. Tricia quickly pulled herself together and wiped away her tears. She then opened the door and greeted William as if he was a scheduled business appointment.

"Have you thought about how we should call off our wedding?" Tricia asked, getting right to the point. She walked over and sat on the couch, and William followed suit.

"I don't want to call off the wedding, Tricia," William said. "I don't want to lose you. I've never felt this way about a woman before. Fear of losing you kept me from telling you about my ex-wife. Please don't call off the wedding."

"When were you going to disclose the fact that you are the father of two children?" Tricia cynically asked.

"Are they troublemakers, too, who also want to harass me?" Pressing her hand forcefully on William's chest, balling, Tricia continued, "Do you have a heart? How could you neglect to mention them? I don't know you at all."

William grabbed Tricia's hand as she tried to raise up off the couch. He pulled her back down and close to him. "Tell me you don't love me, and I will leave. We'll call off this wedding, I'll walk out that door—" He pointed toward the door "—and I'll walk out of your life . . . forever. God knows I don't want to do it. But you tell me you don't love me, and that's exactly what I'll do."

Tricia's eyes began to fill with tears. She couldn't deny her love for William. Sitting there with his arms around her made her feel special, safe, and loved. Sobbing, Tricia confessed her love to William. They then kissed and embraced each other.

Tricia pulled out of the hug and looked into William's eyes. "What are we going to do?"

William began to share his plan with Tricia as if he'd long had everything figured out. "I will talk to your parents and reassure them that I will take care of you and protect you from harm. We can cancel the big wedding, get married at the courthouse, and have our reception as planned. Once we are married, we will move away from here, and my ex will not hassle your family anymore. I know this can work, Tricia."

Tricia exhaled as she sat and thought about her options. She could cancel the wedding and reception and be embarrassed and humiliated, or go ahead with the wedding and pretend everything was perfect. Tricia loved William, and he loved her, and with that final thought, regardless of how she did it, she *would* marry her not-so-perfect man.

"I want to marry you, William, but I agree, we should forego the big wedding," Tricia said, for fear his ex-wife might show up and ruin everything. "I will marry you. But promise me that you won't keep secrets from me ever again."

"I promise!" William said, overjoyed. He pulled her in and hugged her tightly.

Tricia pulled back and glared at William. "Is there anything else I need to know?" Tricia was still skeptical.

William assured her that he had no more secrets and would never hide anything from her again.

Tricia had to inform her parents of her and William's decision to move forward with their marriage, but that instead of their planned wedding, they would get married at a private ceremony at the courthouse in Atlanta. The reception would go on as planned.

After talking with her mom, Tricia felt awful when Mrs. White expressed her disappointment in their decision, but Tricia was insistent that the marriage would go on regardless of how anyone felt about William. She loved him and he was legally divorced.

"A marriage starting out with lies will not work," Mrs. White said, and then begged Tricia to reconsider her decision.

Tricia refused. "Mom, please trust me. I need your help to make my reception a success. Can you do that for me, please?"

Mrs. White hesitated before reluctantly agreeing to assist her daughter.

Tricia and William got married as planned at the courthouse. Laura and John were their only guests. They celebrated with dinner at an elegant restaurant with a delicious steak dinner and beautiful, soft music.

Laura and John surprised the newlyweds with a

reservation at a classy hotel. The happy couple opened the door to a sizable room with a king-size bed covered with a bulky-plush white bedspread with little red hearts. Tricia pulled back the comforter and felt the soft, silky sheets.

When she went into the bathroom, there was an oversized bathtub. A chilled bottle of red wine and two fancy wine glasses sat on the corner of the tub. Everything was perfect. Tricia could only hope this happiness would last forever.

"I hope you'll enjoy a glass of wine with me tonight, Tricia," William said. "Today is the beginning of a lifetime of happiness for us."

William located the corkscrew and opened the bottle of wine. He carefully filled the two glasses. As he handed her the glass of wine, he gazed into her eyes. "To the woman I promise to love forever."

Tricia and William drank the bottle of wine together, danced to their favorite music, enjoying their first night as Mr. and Mrs. Watson.

The Watsons woke up the next morning in awe of a beautiful night together. Tricia felt as if she was on cloud nine and wished she could stay there forever.

"Room service," a voice boomed from the other side of the door.

William and Tricia hadn't ordered any room service. They sat up in bed and stared at each other with confusion. All of a sudden, a thought entered both their minds simultaneously.

"John and Laura," they said in unison, then laughed.

The couple climbed out of the bed and went and answered the door.

"I have breakfast for you," the gentleman wearing a white cook uniform greeted.

John and Laura had thought of everything. The man

walked in smiling and pushing a cart that held a silver coffee pot, a glass pitcher of orange juice, fresh fruits, and a full southern breakfast of grits, eggs, bacon, and toast.

William and Tricia indulged.

"I can't move," Tricia said, holding her belly after finishing breakfast.

They called up the reservation desk and requested a late check out, enjoying their stay and one another's company right up to the last minute.

When the couple returned to Tricia's apartment, they called her parents to inform them they were happily married. Tricia's parents didn't share their enthusiasm but congratulated them nonetheless. Mrs. White assured Tricia everything was on schedule for the reception.

Tricia thanked her mom for supporting her. "We will see you tomorrow. Love you."

Tricia and William used the day to pack for the busy weekend and find gifts for their bridal party. They were at William's house about seven o'clock that evening when his telephone rang. It was his ex-wife calling to tell him that his son had fallen off his bike and was in the emergency room. William explained to Tricia what happened, and said he'd be back as soon as possible. Tricia offered to go along, but William didn't think it was a good idea. He kissed her and hurried out the door as Tricia waited for her husband's return.

Hours passed, and Tricia had not heard from William. At midnight she decided to call a cab to take her back to her apartment to finish packing. Her mind raced with all the things that could be happening with William. She'd only been married a day, and already she was feeling sad and neglected. There was a knock on the door a little past three in the morning. Tricia had barely gotten the door open before William came barreling in.

Sounding a little irritated, William stared at Tricia and asked, "Why didn't you wait at my place? I told you I'd be back as soon as possible."

Tricia became angry. She responded quickly. "I waited five hours for you, and not a phone call. I caught a cab home so I could finish packing. Then another three hours passed and not a word from you. I'm not your girlfriend anymore, I'm your wife, or have you forgotten already?"

William apologized and asked Tricia to forgive him. "I was so worried about Will Jr. that I forgot to call. He fractured his arm and had some bad cuts that needed stitching." He held Tricia in his arms and promised that he'd communicate better in the future.

Tricia calmed down, but was still angry. At that moment, she wished she had listened to her mother as far as marrying William.

The next morning, William placed Tricia's luggage in his car. They drove to his house and they both went inside so he could get his luggage. He carried out his bags while Tricia stayed inside the house to use the bathroom before they hit the road.

No sooner than she exited the bathroom, William's house phone rang. Tricia answered it without thinking.

"Hello."

"This must be Tricia," the voice on the other end of the line said. "What time did William get home last night? Don't think he was at the hospital all that time." Before the woman could say another word, William had entered the house and snatched his phone out of Tricia's hands.

"Hello," he said into the receiver, all while shooting Tricia a cross look. It was clear he wasn't happy about her answering his phone. He had words with his ex and then hung up. "You can't believe anything Sharon says," exclaimed Will. "She's a liar and loves to cause confusion. She didn't want me and doesn't want anyone else to have me."

Tricia couldn't say a word. She nodded her head, acknowledging that she'd heard him. Oh, how Tricia wished she could turn back the hands of time. She suddenly realized she had possibly made a mistake; not just any mistake, but the biggest mistake of her life!

Once on the highway, Tricia began stretching and yawning, pretending to be so tired and sleepy that she couldn't keep her eyes open. Tricia didn't want to talk to William or hear his voice, she just wanted him to disappear from her life. She laid her seat back, kept her eyes closed, fighting back the tears as she wondered how to get out of this mess.

Chapter 7
The Reception

The trip to Charleston was slow and agonizing. William played his music, singing their favorite songs, trying to serenade Tricia without any success. He acted as if he didn't have a clue about how Tricia might be feeling.

When they arrived at her parents' home, Tricia tried to be the happy newlywed, but it wasn't easy. Her sister could tell something was wrong, and even questioned Tricia about it, but Tricia insisted she was only tired.

The newlyweds went to bed early to get some much needed rest. The next morning, Tricia was busy getting ready for the reception. Despite her efforts to pretend otherwise, the excitement was gone.

Tricia in her wedding gown and William in his tuxedo arrived at the reception early, shaking hands and giving hugs to their guests. The wedding party wore dresses and tuxes as well. Not one of William's invited guests showed up. Tricia was able to keep a fake smile on her face as she introduced her husband to family and friends.

The old ladies from church gave their approval of William and complimented how well the couple looked together.

"You sure found a good-looking man," Mrs. Harvey whispered in Tricia's ear. "You'll have some beautiful children together."

Tricia wanted to shout and tell Mrs. Harvey that she'd caused her enough grief and to stay out of her life, but she flashed her phony smile and walked to the next guest.

Tricia watched the clock, wishing she could speed up time. She felt like the leading actress in a movie called

"The Bogus Wedding." After dinner, Tricia's brother and sister gave the toasts.

The DJ called for the bride and groom to the dance floor. William had requested their favorite song. The guests applauded the charismatic moves of the couple when William twirled Tricia around and ended the dance with a dip and a kiss. Tricia was happy when the music stopped. It was then the DJ invited the bridal party and guests to the dance floor.

When it was time to cut the cake, William was very attentive to Tricia. Well aware that everyone was watching them walk toward the cake, William handled Tricia as if she were a precious crystal goblet that would shatter with a little pressure. He looked to be the perfect gentleman.

The reception was winding down, and the crowd gathered around William and Tricia as they prepared to throw the garter and bouquet. The crowd laughed and applauded when William pretended several times to throw the bride's garter to the single men, causing them to run and jump all over the floor.

When Tricia threw her bouquet, she tossed it quickly, feeling sorry for the poor soul who would catch it. They thanked everyone for coming, and then the crowd followed the couple outside and threw rice as they drove away.

Finally, Tricia thought to herself, the reception was over. But her life with William was just getting started.

Chapter 8
Now What?

Mr. and Mrs. William Watson drove to the hotel room that was on reserve for them. Now alone, William confronted Tricia about her attitude toward him. She apologized and blamed her behavior on a migraine headache.

"I need to rest. I took aspirin at the reception. I'll be okay soon," Tricia lied.

Of course, William didn't want to hear this. He left the room and went to the bar. He returned to the hotel room after midnight, very much irritated and ready to give Tricia a piece of his mind. The alcohol helped him express how he felt. William accused Tricia of pretending to be sick and let her know he didn't plan to spend the night comforting her.

"You need to shape up or get out!" William said.

Tricia was furious and shocked to hear William scream at her, but she didn't respond. It frightened her to see him in such a rage. A few minutes later, William passed out on the bed fully dressed, with his shoes still on his feet.

Tricia cried uncontrollably. She saw a side of William she had never seen before. She wanted to run away. Squeezing her pillow close to her body, Tricia fell asleep.

Early the next morning, Tricia felt William's body touching hers. She tried to move away, but he placed his strong arm around her waist and pulled her closer to him. William apologized, this time with tears in his eyes, promising to make up for all the hurt he had caused her.

"I didn't say anything, but I could tell you were upset with me when we left Atlanta," William admitted. "You seemed to despise my presence. I felt rejected. I couldn't do anything to please you. I love you, Tricia. I was hurting and had too much to drink. This is not the weekend I envisioned for us. Please don't shut me out of your life. You must give me a chance to prove my love for you."

Tricia made a promise to give her marriage a chance, although she didn't feel optimistic about it. Tricia realized that God had given her the knowledge and wisdom to make the right decision when it came to moving forward with marrying William. She'd allowed her emotions, pride, fear of being embarrassed, and pressure from others to control her decisions. Now she was suffering the consequences. Tricia blamed herself for her circumstances and pondered the outcome.

She recalled how happy and content she was before she'd said "I do," and wondered if she would ever feel that way again. Reminiscing about all the negative events that had transpired over the past three weeks, Tricia held no hope for the success of William and her marriage. Tricia wished for the days when the old ladies would ask her, "When are you going to tie the knot?" She would gladly say without hesitation, "NEVER!"

"Chosen"
Norma McLauchlin

Introduction

It's been over fifty years since this story began. But needless to say, it's been smoldering inside of me, begging for release throughout the years. Sometimes the desire to tell this story is stronger than others, but yet, I waited for the oxygen required to ignite the ashen coals to a full flame. Join me on the journey as I choose to spread the words of my story.

Chapter 1
The Seed

"But as for you, continue in what you have learned and have become convinced of, because you know those from whom you learned it, and how from infancy you have known the holy Scriptures, which are able to make you wise for salvation through faith in Christ Jesus" (2 Timothy 3:14-15 NIV).

One of the most important aspects of choosing to be free is first choosing to follow Christ. I was six years old when I accepted Christ as my personal Savior. It was one of the most poignant moments in my life.

Prior to my salvation experience, I was a precocious child full of questions. For example, at the age of two, I helped my mother and grandmother churn butter with an old paddle and urn. My favorite part was making designs in the butter using wooden molds. The Fleur di-Lis is still prevalent in many of my design choices today. Then my parents went and purchased a new electric churn. Of course, I had to determine how it worked, for I could not see the inner motor.

Answers from my mother did not satisfy my curiosity. So, I examined the apparatus myself. After having the tip of my pointer finger churned off, I got my answer. There was something inside that big box on top that made the sticks go around. After that experience, churning was no longer my favorite mother-daughter activity. But all was not in vain; I told all who would listen about the mystifying electric churn. Since I remembered hearing my father saying that God could heal anything, I asked God to grow my fingertip back, but I'm still a tip short today.

Always the inquisitive one, I would have my older

sister teach me what she'd learned in school each day. I was enthralled by the stories of Dick and Jane. It was because of one of those readings that I decided I was going to visit the beach. My constant conversation to all who would listen was that God was going to take me to the beach. I was going to wear clothes like in the pictures of the "Dick and Jane" books and build sandcastles.

One day, my aunt told me she and my uncle would be taking my sister and me to the beach that weekend. In my prayers that night, I thanked God, because I had read that if I asked, He would give me the desires of my heart.

True to her word, that Saturday morning, my aunt unveiled the black bathing suits that she had made by hand. They looked just like what Jane had worn to the beach. That afternoon, with a picnic basket in tow, we traveled by car to what I thought was *the* Atlantic Ocean.

After riding for a long while in the backseat of my uncle's big, green car, we arrived at the beach. My sister and I played in the shallow water and built sand castles with wooden spoons and tin cans. It was a glorious day— the pages inside a book had come to life!

It was not until much later in life I was told this memorable experience took place on the beach of the Haw River, which meanders through my hometown. But it didn't matter—the seed of salvation had been planted and watered.

To this day, the water and ocean still fill my spirit with the awesomeness of God. I do my best work after experiencing the sunrise and offering praise to God, for I don't know who else could have made such splendor!

Chapter 2
The Foundation

Jesus said, "Let the little children come to me, and do not hinder them, for the kingdom of heaven belongs to such as these" (Matthew 19:14 NIV).

As a youngster, I followed my father everywhere. As a Baptist church deacon, he was a pillar in our community. Not only did he visit the sick in the community, but he supported those who sometimes needed an additional helping hand. In our conversations about why we helped people in our community, my father explained how as Christians, we were to practice the Beatitudes that are found in Matthew 5:1-12. Also, since most of the sermons I heard were about how not to go to hell, I asked questions about hell *and* heaven. Although the answers were not always satisfactory, I decided it would be better to go to the beautiful city in the sky rather than the everlasting pit of fire.

The day I went to the altar and expressed my decision to become "saved" was a wonderful day for me as well as my family. My baptism was planned for the following Sunday; however, I refused to be baptized in the usual dirty, brown water of the creek. I requested a pool of clear water. So, my father arranged for a baptism pool at one of the sister churches.

The night before the event, my hair was straightened and rolled with brown paper. I'd wear my hair full of curls for my special day. My parents purchased me a new white dress with ruffles and lace, and white patent leather shoes that were to be worn with frilly, white socks.

Dressed in a much too large baptismal robe on that bright, sunny, Sunday morning, my mother continuously instructed me not to get my hair wet. I wasn't sure how I was to accomplish that, being I was getting baptized . . . in a pool of water. But by the time I stepped into the pool, my hair was covered with a swimming cap over a plastic bag. For extra security, I also wore a shower cap underneath a white towel that was tied snuggly around my head. When I was presented before the church that morning as saved and baptized, I stood proudly in my white finery with my shiny, tight curls still in place. To this day, I'm not sure how I withstood the vise-like feeling surrounding my head during my baptism. I recall looking out amongst the congregation, and seeing some members with tear-filled eyes. I don't know if my mother's tears were of joy for my salvation or for the mere fact that my hair was still intact.

Growing up as an avid reader, I always read the Bible. I had plenty of questions about the scriptures, but I believed with childlike certainty that God was the Savior of my soul. The question that sticks out most in my memory is that of God's curse of the serpent for tempting Eve to sin against Him. After reading that story numerous times, while accompanying my father to Bible study, I asked if the serpent walked on earth before God cursed it. The Bible clearly stated that the punishment was to crawl on its belly. My logical conclusion was that in order for God to punish the serpent in that manner, it had to have walked. Of course, since that question had never been posed to the group before, they had no answer. It was suggested, though, that since I was only six years old, I should study with children my own age.

Another question I pondered was if the children of Adam and Eve married each other. I read that after being kicked out of the garden, Adam and Eve were to populate the earth. Well, of course, in my limited thinking, I knew one didn't marry their brother or sister, but how else was this to happen? Back to the grown-ups' Bible study I went for answers. Again, no specific answer was provided.

My father explained that it was not that the elders in Bible study did not want to answer my questions, but that most of them simply were not able to interpret or explain the answers to my particular questions.

I was equally as inquisitive when it came to school as I was in church. Since there was no kindergarten class during that time, my elementary years consisted of first through eighth grade. In the all-black public school, my teachers cared about me as an individual. They knew my parents, grandparents, aunts, and uncles. I still know each of my teachers and have personal memories of how they affected my life.

One of my fondest memories is of my third-grade teacher, Mrs. Gravely. I was always the shortest student in my class and was often picked on because of it. But one day, Mrs. Gravely had me go to the soda machine in the big hall to get her a soda. I told her I could not reach the money slot, so I could not get it. But she smiled and said, "That's why I'm sending Isaac with you." Isaac was the tallest student in class.

When we got to the machine, I gave Isaac the money, which he put into the machine and pressed the button. I picked up the soda, placing it in the bag I was instructed to carry it in back to our classroom in the little hall.

Isaac and I delivered the soda to Mrs. Gravely. Upon receiving it she smiled and said, "God made both of you unique.

You need each other to accomplish your goals in life." I still live by the wisdom of Mrs. Gravely.

The years before integration in schools were what set

the standard for my life. It was God's wisdom through each of my teachers from first through eighth grade that laid the foundation for my education. In hindsight, as an educator myself, that is what I seek for students today. It is because of my educators' teachings that I feel free to reach beyond the textbooks to my students.

Chapter 3
The Decision

"Trust in the Lord with all of your heart and lean not on your own understanding; in all your ways acknowledge him, and he will make your paths straight" (Proverbs 3:5-6 NIV).

In choosing freedom through choosing Christ, I found that I could not do so without also choosing faith. My opportunity to test my faith came during the turbulent sixties. Similar to the times of Esther, there was racial conflict in the southern United States. African Americans felt that they were not being educated on a level playing field with white students. Mainly, this issue was because black students were taught from dated curricula. To address this educational void, many black communities throughout the South had integrated the white schools. The NAACP in my hometown was also seeking a solution to the education issue.

During my eighth-grade year in 1965, my parents were asked if I could integrate the only white school in my county. As members of the NAACP, they said yes and I was approached with the idea one night during a 4-H meeting (a youth organization with the mission of "engaging youth to reach their fullest potential"). Leaders from the local NAACP explained that they had singled me out for this assignment. They told me that they knew I could withstand the repercussions of attending the school.

At the time, I was unaware that a conversation I'd had with one of my closest friends was another part of the reason I'd been handpicked for this task. A few weeks previously, I'd talked my friend out of fighting physically, and using her head instead. The conversation with my friend took place late one evening when she'd called and told me that several of the students at the school we attended wanted to fight her. While sitting at the island in my parents' kitchen/den talking on a party line phone, I suggested that she not fight.

"We are too intelligent to fight physically," I told her. "We are educated young ladies, and we can fight with our brains. Words are better than fists."

She listened without interruption as I went on to share with her that if God could calm a raging sea with the words, "Peace be still," we could find words that would diffuse confrontations and find peace in the situation. Little did I know, that conversation was overheard by my father and shared with hers, who happened to be one of the NAACP leaders that approached me.

It was that shared account of this one conversation, along with my academic achievement, which led to me being chosen to take up the charge for integrating County Schools. I had been chosen as the individual to integrate the local white high school in Wentworth, North Carolina. I had been chosen to lead the change from an inferior education for black students in County in North Carolina to an education equal with white students. However, this decision was not made easily.

There was much debate between my family and myself, my teachers, and most importantly at that time, my peers. I distinctly remember standing at the kitchen sink in my family's kitchen talking with my father about the decision to integrate the white high school. I told him that I thought God had something He wanted me to do for my people, but that I didn't want to go. I wanted to go with my friends to the black high school. I wanted my entire high school experience to include a social life with people who looked like me, not people who didn't want me to step foot in the same building as them.

Since there was only one black high school, all the African American students in the county attended it. I had been excited about attending the high school since I could remember. My friends and I had it all planned out. We would take the same classes, join the same clubs, and try out for the cheerleading team. It didn't matter that we had to get up before dark, get on the bus in the dark, ride past the white high school, arrive at the elementary school, then catch the bus to the all-black high school and start classes by eight in the morning. Not to mention then reverse the entire process, and in the winter, arrive back home near dark. Since I didn't know anything different, I wanted to go. It was deemed as the "right of passage" to high school, and I desperately wanted to experience it.

It seemed that everyone said that I was the best choice to integrate, and I had to do it for my people. Some of them toyed with my conscience by saying that my going was the route for a better education for *all* black students in The County. Others suggested that I was the only eighth grader with the grades and intestinal fortitude to see the venture through. Still, others maintained that my father was a pillar in the black community and well respected in the white community, so that would help pave the way for me. Some even suggested that I would not experience as much name-calling because of my medium brown skin, and hair that was not too "nappy."

My friends, however, triggered my emotions by continuously reminding me of what I would be giving up mostly—my social life. I would have no one to date or hang out with at the white high school, because they would be afraid to be seen with me.

The opposing parties showed their feelings by burning a cross in the field across the street from my home and by threatening my father. But little did they know, they were dealing with what the black community leader called a "Tucker." My dad, Oscar Otis Tucker Jr., declared that we would not be intimidated, and our people would get an equal education. He instilled in me that the Tucker name had meaning and power. I was to live up to all that went with it; integrity, honesty, high moral values, strong work ethics, confidence in who I was, and always standing proudly with my head up.

Making the decision whether to "take up the cross" and attend the white school filled my mind and soul with turmoil. I had seen what the power of the water hoses did to marchers. I had witnessed the KKK lined up on their horses ready to terrorize black families. However, I sought God throughout the decision-making process and felt He agreed with everyone who wanted me to go. It was not about me, but about the children following me. Although it was with great apprehension, I said to my parents, "I'm scared, but I will go." So, for the next four years of my life, I, with the support of my community and parents, was in pursuit of the elusive better education for my people.

Unlike Esther, who had months to prepare to meet Haman, the summer prior to my freshman year of high school was spent being briefed and prepped on how to act, what to wear, and how to respond in different situations at my new high school. The main thing I remember was what I was to wear on the first day of school.

Since it was a common belief that black people liked the color red, to not instigate name-calling, I was not to wear anything red while at school. Therefore, the colors of my clothes were basic autumn colors; blue, brown, tan, or a combination of the three.

The day of reckoning finally came. I was ready. In my burgundy skirt and floral top picked out by the Home

Extension agent (the county representative who provided "expert" information to the women in the county), I waited for the bus. I will never forget the feelings of fear, despair, and hopelessness that morning. I felt like the sacrificial lamb being led to slaughter. I remember asking myself if this was how the people in the Bible felt when they were waiting on deliverance. But the bus stopped, and to my surprise, the front seat was vacant, so I took it. I was told that the front seat behind the driver was my seat. I sat alone on that same seat for three years without incident. I actually ended up driving a school bus during my senior year.

During the ride, I prayed that God would be with me and deliver me from all hurt and danger that I imagined would meet me at the school. After fifteen of the most excruciating minutes of my life (a much shorter ride to school than it would have been had I attended the black high school), the bus arrived at school to a host of cameras and spectators. The bus stopped at the front steps of an imposing, historical-looking building with Palladian windows and what I thought were thousands of steps leading to the front entrance. My new education facility looked more like an old museum than any school I'd ever witnessed. To my surprise and amazement, all the students remained seated while I was escorted off the bus and up those many steps, without incident, into the beginning of my high school journey.

Chapter 4
In the Lion's Den

"At my first defense, no one came to my support, but everyone deserted me. May it not be held against them. But the Lord stood at my side and gave me strength, so that through me the message might be fully proclaimed and all the Gentiles might hear it. And I was delivered from the lion's mouth. The Lord will rescue me from every evil attack and will bring me safely to his heavenly kingdom. To him be glory forever and ever. Amen." (2 Timothy 4:16-18 NIV).

My mentally traumatic freshman year began with the school principal showing me around the school. He explained my class schedule and showed me where my classes would be held. The principal implied that he did not expect any trouble, but if I had any, I was to let him know immediately. Little did he know, I had been primed in the art of passive behavior. I was not to respond with violence by word or deed. Therefore, for four years, I never complained or reported any negative behavior to that principal.

There were no students to greet me. No welcome groups pretending to be friends could be found. Although now I think my parents, the principal, and other involved leaders made the decision that to make my transition as normal as possible, there was to be little fanfare. It was the beginning of the loneliest period of my life.

My ninth-grade year was certainly not what I had dreamed of it being. Inside the building, with circus animal murals painted on the wall, was another set of steps leading to the basement floor where the cafeteria, as well as some of my classes, was located. These steps became my nemesis. No matter how many times I reached the bottom, spit would come from the upper landing and hit me on the top of my head while someone called me the N-word. Even when I waited until I saw no one around to go down the stairs, most days I was spit on. You know, maybe that's why the texture of my hair on the top of my head is different. The top is softer and the coils are not as tight as on the sides and back. Makes me wonder if there is a hidden ingredient in saliva that changes the texture of hair.

I would go to the janitor's closet, where I ate lunch each day, and Mr. and Mrs. Purcell, the custodians who were also African American, would help me clean my hair. At the end of each day, I had the tedious task of washing and straightening my thick, unmanageable hair. It was because of this daily spit cleaning that I got my hair permanently straightened by a hairdresser who chemically straightened and cut my hair to a shorter style that would be easier to manage. Unfortunately, managing my high school years wouldn't be as easy.

Chapter 5
I am Chosen

"The nations will see your vindication, and all kings your glory; you will be called by a new name that the mouth of the Lord will bestow" (Isaiah 62:2 NIV).

It was during my freshman year that I heard God call me by His name for me. After one of those highly stressful days that included everything from being called names, to being spat on and having a cross burned in my yard, I contemplated not continuing this educational journey.

My parents were very proud that their daughter was chosen for such a time as this. They didn't hesitate to let people know that I was the one changing history for our people in The County. Since I didn't want to disappoint my parents or the community leaders, I never explained all that was happening to me at the white school. But it became almost unbearable.

I told my father I was leaving the school and going to the all-black high school. I told him I thought God had a higher calling for me at the black school. Of course, he told me to pray and think about it. "You know why you made the decision to go," my father said to me. "You said that God told you to go. Remember, God is not the author of confusion, and He does not lie. Either He said it, or He did not."

I decided to take up the mantle of integrating the school. Being a Tucker, I could not go back on a promise, for my word was my bond. The only way out was through an act of God.

Again, standing alone in our kitchen, looking out the window over the sink with my mother's starter plants, I tried to find the Peace of God. I tried to reason with myself if what I was doing would have an impact on the lives of those following me. Was this feeling of desolation and loneliness worth the conflict I was experiencing?

While praying and telling God I was leaving, God spoke to me. "Norma, my Chosen One, you were chosen for this job by man *and* by Me. It's not about you, it's about my people. You will be alright. You are able to partially see the vision and understand what is needed to make this a success. You will make it through. I am with you and will never leave you. No physical harm will come to you. I AM with you."

There is no sweeter sound than when I hear my Heavenly Father call me Chosen, for He is not one to lie. Therefore, I knew beyond a shadow of a doubt that He was going to be with me, and that everything was truly going to be all right. And when God said to me, "You know I will fulfill my promises," it was even further confirmation. So, from that day, in my family's kitchen, I put aside my fear, and continued the journey for equal education for the black children of The County.

Two additional black students joined me during my sophomore year. It was during this time I realized the white race had color stereotypes for the African American race. One day after PE, while in the showers, a red-headed, heavy-set girl from the low economic side of the tracks told me that she could tolerate me, but not the other student, because she was as black as a crow. She thought that "people that black could not be trusted."

It was only through quick prayer that I was able to continue to practice my mantra of "fight with brains, not fists." I told her that like her, our race had different eye and hair colors, and not all blacks were all the same. "We have unique features, including skin color," I said to her. "Trust is not dependent on the color of a person's skin, but the content of their character." Again, I did not let ignorance prevail.

Of course, since I was black, I was expected to play sports.

Needless to say, sports were not something at which I excelled. But in my sociology class, my teacher explained the evolution and said that the Negroid race had longer bone structure, and that's why they were so good at sports as opposed to whites, who had more brain power. Of course, I asked the class to look at my arms and to decide if this theory held up. Again, the height issue arose, and it was decided that I must be an anomaly, because the only thing known by the white students was that black people were only good for sports and working in the fields.

By my senior year, the school was fully integrated. There was a busload of black students matriculating from first through twelfth grade. The only relief I had was that I was allowed to accompany my younger sister to the black high school social events. Although I enjoyed myself at the basketball and football games, I was taunted by my own race for using the King's English. I was told that I thought I was white. So, needless to say, I quickly learned to operate in both worlds.

At school, I spoke and acted like a student preparing for a future in society, and at social activities, I resorted to fitting in with the black community. My sister would keep me abreast of the latest lingo and dances. The best part was that I could wear bright colored clothes.

When I went to the theater with the kids at the black school, I had to sit in the balcony, known as the "Crow's Nest." However, when I went to the same theater during field trips with my high school class, I sat with them on the main floor.

Graduation day was one of the best days of my life.

God had delivered me from the lion's den. Hallelujah! I felt free. I had fulfilled my obligation to God and to man. Little did I know; my life obligations had only just begun.

Chapter 6
My Purpose

"And we know that all things God works for good of those who love him, who are called according to his purpose" (Romans 8:28 NIV).

Even though I had finished high school, served in the military, gotten married, earned degrees from both an HBCU and two major predominately white universities, and taught school on the Navajo Indian Reservation, the HBCU and one of the major universities, I was still not confident of what God wanted me to do with the remainder of my life. I was unsure of my purpose.

It was not until later in life that I identified and understood my spiritual gifts. Although I unknowingly used them in the secular work environment, I felt somewhat at odds with myself in church. I was always able to use my drive for independence and creative ingenuity to provide income for myself. From the age of six, I always found ways to earn money. In summers, using my father's push lawn mower, I would walk through the white neighborhoods seeking lawn jobs. In the winter, I would ask if there was a need to clean bathrooms or houses. During my teen years, I earned money by working on the white man's tobacco farm when not working the family tobacco farm. As I mentioned earlier, my senior year in high school, I drove the school bus. Ironically, I picked up the students from the black neighborhood and transported the nonintegrated bus of students to the integrated school.

In my jobs in the military, and as a faculty member at the local university, I excelled in my endeavors. I quickly moved up the ranks in the US Women's Army Core. After enduring the pain and sorrow of integrating the white public school, I worked at a predominately black college and university. It was there that my philosophy became, "show students you care, and they will excel."

I realized it's not about the textbooks, but about mentoring. Those students who had someone in their corner, especially during their freshmen year—in spite of low SAT scores, in spite of coming from low economic backgrounds, and in spite of being a first-generation student—were successful in their endeavors. They only needed the same type of teachers I had in elementary school; teachers who applied Godly wisdom, along with book knowledge; teachers who could give real-world examples of white writers' textbook situations.

During my tenure at Fayetteville State University, my creative and innovative expertise were welcomed and supported. I developed and implemented several programs surrounding the mentoring of college students. It was not until my husband and I begin a ministry that I felt like I didn't belong.

After planning, organizing, and implementing the New Life Bible Fellowship of America, I seemed not to be able to find my footing. I thought that something was wrong with me. It was customary that the wife of a pastor either supported her husband by playing the piano, singing in the choir, or providing meals. Of course, although I was capable of doing these things and did them, I found no joy in doing them, often telling my husband that I was unhappy with the situation. There had to be something that I could do, or somewhere I fit in.

Don't get me wrong; I didn't hate doing the things I did to show my support as the pastor's wife, but I wasn't passionate about them. I was content doing what the men normally did, which was operations. I was happy when designing and implementing programs that would bring more people to the Kingdom.

I continued to pray and ask God what else He had for me to do. I'd already accomplished the assignment of integrating my high school—now what? Surely, I was not doing whatever *it* was. Then one day I completed the Spiritual Gifts Assessment Inventory, a personal assessment designed to identify a person's spiritual gifts and areas they could use in God's environment. I discovered that my spiritual gifts were in the lines of being an administrator, exhorter, and giver. Eureka! Hallelujah! There was nothing wrong with me after all. Those were the areas in which I excelled and should have been operating in.

After reading Rick Warren's *The Purpose Driven Life*, I had another "Aha!" moment. Not only did I know my spiritual gifts and how to operate in them within the church, but I knew how to apply them to specific goals and responsibilities within my own Christian walk and for the building of the Kingdom. For example, instead of running around willy-nilly trying to be a visionary in everything, I found that my gift fit better with the purpose of evangelism.

After studying the purpose of discipleship, I exhorted others through Bible studies, encouraging the ladies that I counseled to understand that God had a higher purpose for their lives. The feeling of being truly free to operate in my gifts was . . . well . . . freeing. As a matter of fact, unearthing my gifts was one of the most freeing moments of my life. I am now and forever free to dream and visualize! I am free to plan! I am free to encourage others one-on-one! I am free to give and share!

And most importantly, all these gifts are freely given to me from God through the Holy Spirit. I am free and expected to walk in my purpose while here on earth to build God's Kingdom. I love God for that!

Now, all I had left to do was to identify the right path for my purpose.

Chapter 7
The Integration Paradox

*"If anyone causes one of these little ones—those who believe in me—
to stumble, it would be better for them to have a large millstone hung
around their neck and to be drowned in the depths of the sea."*
(Matthew 18:6 NIV).

Coming full circle, I used my purpose for ministry to start
a Christian school. The irony of this venture is that it has a
predominately black student body. My overarching
mission is to not lose one child to the world. The mission
is operationalized by meeting each student where they are
academically and matching the curricula that best fits their
educational need.

You are probably asking why the person who
integrated a white school would start a predominately
black Christian school. First, by the sixth grade, my son
had not been educated by a teacher who looked like him.
It was when he was to enter a public middle school that I
became aware that his school's environment was not
totally conducive to learning. When my son came home
and announced I was not to worry about him attending
school, because he had found a gang that would help look
after him at school, I knew he would never set foot in that
school again.

Second, I constantly asked myself if the struggle of
integration was the best for my people. Based on my
experience, I would not wish my high school years on any
child. I believe a student needs more than book knowledge
to be prepared for society. In my opinion, there needs to
be social and cultural integration as well.

Also, today, based on my experience and
conversations with my peers, it appears that ingenuity,

creativity, and innovativeness has been drained from us as a race of people. Where are our leaders and our creators? Our students don't interact with a teacher who looks and thinks like them for most of their educational journey. The question becomes; were we really better educated even with the inferior curricula? Did the love and respect from caring teachers make the educational field level with those of the other race, in spite of the materials used to teach us?

Today, I realize I have come full circle in my thinking about the education of children. I find that nurture wins over new curriculum or highly degreed teachers. When a child is told, "You can do it!" or "You are smart," the sky becomes the limit for them.

I began to understand that it was not the textbooks that were the reason for a better education, but the love and respect teachers showed to their students. I still remember my first-grade teacher, Mrs. King, who answered my just-learning-how-to-write cursive written letters during the summer of my first-grade year. Mrs. Noble taught me that it was my duty to assist my peers who did not catch on as quickly as I did. Mrs. Gravely taught me that a person's stature is not measured by inches.

After using the judo techniques taught to me by my WWII veteran father on a boy in my class, my fourth-grade teacher explained that when boys teased and hit girls, it was their way of showing their positive feeling for girls, and I should not fight them and call them names. Instead, she told me to be patient with them, because one day the boys would learn how to express themselves better.

The fifth grade brought my first encounter with health and weight management. Mrs. Foye encouraged the girls to drink a cup of warm lemon water each day at lunch. She explained that this mixture would keep us healthy, youthful, and beautiful. The sixth, seventh, and eighth grades were filled with teachers giving advice on how girls were to carry themselves, proper etiquette, and how to respond to each other. Mrs. Williams, Mrs. Banks, and Mr. Jones were instrumental in my personal development and helped shape my self-esteem as well as self-respect. Mrs. Gravely, however, became my role model. I still tell people that, "God made tall people to serve short people." That's the reason I married a tall man. He's my top shelf guy.

It is with these memories that I govern New Life Christian Academy. Each student is shown love and respect daily. Faculty and staff go more than the extra mile to ensure that the needs of the entire student body are met. The New Life Trifecta is the school, home, and church working together to produce successful children. Through its twenty years of existence, students who were predicted and labeled to never be successful have learned to read and earn a high school diploma. They have gone on to lead productive lives as citizens adding value to their communities.

There have been many ups and downs, from being the only predominately black Christian school in Cumberland County, to having to compete with many start-ups and charter schools. I believe that nothing happens by chance. I know that the school was a God thing for me. So even though the adversity has been great, we are still prevailing. Since I believe that God revealed and prepared me for my current assignment of helping minority students excel in today's world, I will continue to walk and operate daily in my calling and purpose.

Chapter 8
Full Circle

"In Him we were also chosen, having been predestined according to the plan of him who works out everything in conformity with the purpose of his will, in order that we, who were in the first hope in Christ, might be for the praise of his glory" (Ephesians 1:11-12 NIV).

Although my faith has been tested several times since my initial assignment from God as a teenager (which at the time I felt was the ultimate test of faith), faith is still one of the strongest areas of my life. I believe that nothing is too big for God. This has not always been the case; however, my problem was and still is at times that I don't always have the patience to wait for God to work out what I know He is going to do in my life, or in the lives of others. But the peace of God enables me to know that He is sovereign and He is in control of my life. He will always be with me. I know He answers prayers. Although the answer may not be the one I want, He will answer. I only have to ask.

I get goosebumps when I think of how God's mind is so much higher than mine, and His ways so much broader than I can even imagine. It's astounding to now realize how He puts His plans in action. It amazes me even more to know that He had these plans for me from the beginning of time; plans to give me hope and a future. It is this knowledge that continues to broaden my faith. With God in charge, I can step out on faith and carry out His will.

As I unite my earthly purpose with God's purpose for me, I can only watch His sovereign works in awe. Whenever my faith is tested, I only think about the awesomeness of God and how He has chosen me for this ultimate purpose.

Today, looking back over my past, I ask myself, "Could this have been God's plan for me all along?" In His sovereignty, were my experiences in elementary school, the white high school, the military, the colleges and universities I attended, and work on the Navajo Indian Reservation preparing me for a greater work for the black children in my future? Was it about learning to apply the scripture of "suffer little children" to a much boarder base? Was He preparing me to reach students to intercede on behalf of black children who have been given up on by others, causing them to believe that they can never achieve?

Was I to provide the fulfillment of the need for students who are so smart that they are not challenged in the classroom? Was I really chosen to level the playing field for minority students today? Was the explanation given by God in our conversation during my high school freshmen year being fulfilled. For now, I understand more fully what He meant when He said, "Norma, my Chosen One, you were chosen for this job by man *and* by Me. It's not about you, it's about my people. You will be all right. You are able to partially see the vision and understand what is needed to make this a success. You will make it through. I am with you and will never leave you. No physical harm will come to you. I AM with you".

Based on that conversation, I now see how all the situations in my life were preparing me for such a time as this. Although the vision is much clearer now, is it complete? Is there more for me to do?

Well, God is sovereign and my faith is strong, so I am ready for whatever plans God has for me and I freely choose to walk in my God-given purpose until He says otherwise.

This Is Chosen

"Silent Tears"
Florence Levy

It was hiding deep in the ocean;
Calm waves waiting to rip the sea.

After the stormy wind raged outside, the moon shone
bright, and the rainbow burst from behind the dark
clouds.

It was hidden in the murky water, under the logs forgotten
long ago.

Fish came out of rivers to spatter the
clean, fresh water running down the
cheek.

A frown has turned inside out.
It was there all the time, you know;
A secret that would not show.

Come, now, let's dance the night away.
Slippery feet sliding on the soft green grass,
tossing worries and fears in the air.

The roses in the garden grew up, and the fragrance is so

sweet.

Oh, how good it feels; those silent tears.

"Trouble Don't Last Always"
Suzetta Perkins

Chapter 1
Helping Hands Get Dirty Sometimes

It wasn't an isolated incident. The scars that broke Malika's spirit were meant for her; an unsolicited target had been placed on her back. Time and again, she faced her tormentors and repeatedly begged for them to stop the harassment. Her bruised heart couldn't take much more.
Fifty-two-year-old Malika Price was a beautiful woman, inside and out. She was a full-figured woman who dressed in the best designer suits and wore her Christian Louboutin shoes that boasted five-inch heels, with no regrets. Large, brown eyes were set in her round, milk chocolate-colored complexioned face, and her hair—a reddish-brown, lace-front wig—was her crowning glory. At five feet and ten inches tall, she carried it all well.

However, Malika's beauty extended well beyond the physical. She gave willingly of herself as she motivated, encouraged, and mentored young, black, teenage males to excel in STEM courses—science and math—with thoughts of continuing their education beyond high school. She spent lots of time with them, having groomed her own son, who was an aerospace engineer at NASA, working on probing satellites.

Life, as she knew it, took a sudden, ugly turn. Whispers in the night—*let not your good be evil spoken of*—haunted her. It was the devil gloating, but God knew her heart. The devil tried to take her good work in the community and strangle her by allowing false allegations to slander her name. And Malika remembered the day when all the mud-slinging started all too well. It was late fall . . . almost six months to the day. The leaves had turned dirty brown and ruddy red. Six years into Malika's mentoring program, a petite woman entered her facility, Teach One, Reach One Academy, while Malika stood, returning a book to its spot on the shelf.

The woman wore a pair of black jeans and an oversized, white t-shirt with white flip-flops flopping on her feet that she dragged across the concrete floor. Cornrow braids blazed a trail across the woman's head, causing her to look even more intimidating, giving credence to the way she entered the room. Her vibe was on stink, although Malika didn't know how foul until the accusation came rumbling out of the woman's mouth.

"Excuse me," the woman said. "I'm looking for a Ms. Price."

"I'm Ms. Price," Malika said in response, swinging around from the bookshelf to face the woman.

"You are mentoring my son, Justus, and he informed me that you put your hands on him."

"What do you mean, 'I put my hands on him?'" Malika said, raising both hands in front of her. "I've patted his head a few times to acknowledge that he was doing a fantastic job. There's no harm in that." At least in Malika's opinion, not enough harm to cause the woman to be in such an uproar.

"That's not what he told me." The woman smacked

her lips as she shifted all of her weight to one side and threw her hand on her hips.

"Ms. . . ." Malika paused, realizing the woman had not introduced herself by name.

"My name is Celeste, and Justus Miller is my son. That's all you need to know." The woman looked Malika up and down, almost daring her to investigate any further.

"Ms. Celeste, Justus is a good student and is doing quite well. His math teacher wouldn't have sent him to this program if she hadn't seen Justus' ability to go beyond what he's been doing in her class."

Celeste stared at Malika, unconcerned about her son's ability to excel in his studies. "I didn't come here to talk about what Justus is going to be when he grows up. His life has already been determined. He's going to be like every other black kid in our neighborhood, sell drugs, get shot by the cops—"

Malika's mouth dropped open. "Wow! What a crazy thing to say. All children don't sell drugs, and while the future may look bleak for you, that doesn't mean it has to be. Even in the worst of circumstances, many children have been able to go beyond the stereotypical atmosphere they were born in to become productive citizens and make a name for themselves. It's a shame that you don't have the same kind of interest in your son's ability to excel in his education."

Celeste bunched her lips and pointed her finger at Malika. "First of all, don't you dare tell me that I don't have an interest in my son's education. You don't know me like that. Like I said, this visit isn't about how smart Justus is, but about you touching my son where your hands don't belong."

"Now, you listen. I have never been inappropriate with your son, so if he's told you that I've done so, he's lying to you."

"You calling my son a liar?" Celeste glared at Malika. "He wouldn't ever tell me something like you putting your hands on him if you hadn't done it." She pointed an accusing finger at Malika. "I will have you kicked out of this program."

"I'm giving back to my community. What are you doing? I'm utilizing a lot of my own money, not to mention my time, to help young, black boys to excel and not be a statistic. I'm giving them my all," Malika said with passion, "so they can matriculate through high school with good grades, go on to college, and hopefully become successful doctors, scientists, researchers, you name it."

"All while you're using that as a cover to molest young boys because your fat behind can't get nobody." She looked Malika up and down with disgust. "Yeah, I said it. You're wearing those fancy clothes to attract these boys' attention, while pretending to school them on becoming something you know darn well they ain't got a chance in the world of becoming." She let out a tsk. "Feeding them false hopes and dreams just so you can get your rocks off."

Now it was Malika who had a look of disgust on her face. "It's black mothers like you who give the black race a bad name. I'm giving my time to help your child, and you've got the nerve to step to me, talking some nonsense about me touching your child. If I touched him anywhere, it would be his brain."

"I'm taking your butt to the school board. Touch that!" Celeste said, then let out a 'harrumph.'"

"You still haven't told me exactly where I supposedly touched your son."

"If you can stand there and look me in the eye as if you don't have any idea of what I'm talking about, you deserve what's coming to you." Celeste's tone was laced with venom and hate.

"You're the one who came in here with the accusation. It's only fair that I understand what it is that I'm supposed to have done. So, I'm asking you again, where did I supposedly touch your son?"

"Since you making me say it, you touched his privates," Celeste said. "There, does that get some kind of rise out of you or something? To force me to have to say it?"

Malika tried her best to maintain her composure, but she could no longer do so after hearing the words that had come out of Celeste's mouth. "And he's lying!" Malika's hand went in the air and pointed toward the door. The unmitigated gall for this woman to step to her with some cockamamie story that she'd molested her son. "Now, get out of my facility before I throw you out."

"Tuh." Celeste flung her hand and shooed it at Malika. "You haven't heard the last of me." Celeste twirled around and moved swiftly across the room, her flip-flops slapping the floor. She turned back around before exiting the room, throwing up her hand, and pointing her finger at Malika. "You will pay for what you've done."

The room was quiet upon Celeste's exit, and Malika fell into the first chair nearest to where she had stood. Tears gushed from her eyes. It was hard to fathom that all her efforts had come to this.

Malika sat a few minutes longer. A smile eventually emerged on her face. She tossed images around in her head of the young boys she'd mentored, seeing them in the future as they walked across the stage to receive their diplomas. And as easy as the images had come, they quickly evaporated. Then she saw Justus' face.

And then she remembered.

Chapter 2
What Are You Trying to Do?

It was four-thirty in the afternoon. The sun would set in less than an hour. Only a handful of boys came to the center that day. Malika was excited about leaving a little early so she could go shopping for a Halloween costume for a party she planned to attend. Before she got up to leave, Justus Miller came through the door.

Justus was about as tall as Malika, give or take a couple of inches. His hair was shaved on the sides and the back, while the top was a wooly afro. His skin was ebony with a purple tint, and his teeth a soft white. Basketball was his sport of choice, and for a junior in high school, his hands and fingers were so large and long that when he palmed the basketball, they reminded Malika of a spider web. Many times, he'd come to the center bouncing a ball after coming from practice. Today was no different.

"Hey, Justus," Malika greeted. "You're much later than usual." She looked down at her watch and then back up at Justus. "I was planning to leave in a few minutes."

"I . . . I do have a problem that I need your help with this afternoon," Justus said. "It's a trigonometry problem that I can't seem to figure out."

"Okay, sure. You go ahead and sit down at the table." Malika pointed to the table she did most of the instruction with the boys at. "I'll be over in a sec." Malika headed over to her desk and retrieved her purse.

Justus opened his book while Malika painted her lips and brushed back her hair. She dotted her neck with perfume from a pocket spray she had in her purse. As soon as she and Justus were finished with his problem, she was going to head straight out and she wanted to be ready.

Malika hovered over Justus while he went over the

problem and identified the area where he was having trouble. Moving in closer to take a better look, Malika outlined on paper the course Justus should take in solving the problem, and identified why it was so.

While Malika had basically mapped out the problem for Justus, she noticed that his concentration was elsewhere.

"Do you need me to go over it again?" Malika asked, her arms now folded as she stood behind Justus.

"No, I got it," Justus said matter of fact. He stuck his notepad inside his book, closed it, and stood up.

"What's wrong, Justus?" Malika asked with a look of concern on her face.

"Nothing's wrong, Ms. Price. I uh, I want to ask you a question." Justus looked down at the ground as he began to wring his hands.

Puzzled, Malika stared at Justus as he prepared his question. "What is it?"

Justus held his head back up slightly and then pulled it up as if he had obtained a bit of courage from someplace in the universe. Leaving his book on the table, he inched toward Malika, her hands still folded across her stomach.

"What is it?" Malika asked again, now confused as Justus took steps to shorten the distance between them.

Before Malika could react, Justus grabbed and tried to kiss her.

"What are you doing?" Malika asked in disgust, pushing him away.

"I like you, Ms. Price. I dream about you all the time," Justus admitted, seemingly confused as to why she would reject him.

"That's not right, Justus. I'm your teacher. I'm here to give you guidance. Besides, I'm much too old for you."

"But when I smelled your perfume, I thought . . . that maybe you were feeling me the way I was feeling you."

"You thought I put that perfume on for you?"

"You are pretty. And I like big women." Justus gave Malika the onceover, which made her feel even more uncomfortable than she was already feeling.

"Okay, Justus. That's enough. Stop it right now. I can't continue to mentor you." Malika shook her head while she walked over to her desk, which was as far as she could get away from Justus without actually leaving the room. "You've done so well here, but this assertion that you like me will cause a conflict. I'll see if I can find another program that you can fit into."

"No, I don't want to be tutored by anyone else. I want us to run away and have sex like those girls that were in the news, who ran off with their teachers. I really like you. If I can just . . . just hug . . ."

Malika stomped her foot. "Get out, now, Justus. Get out now." Panting loud, she pointed toward the door. "I'm not going to run away with you or anyone else. If you leave, I won't tell anyone that this even happened. I'm going to erase it from my mind this very moment."

Not appearing to be in too much of a hurry, Justus began to gather his things without saying another word. He backed away, snatched his book off the table, and left the room with a scowl on his face.

Malika continued to stand. Dumbfounded, she sat, crossed her legs, and tried to digest what had just taken place. Even though she had promised to erase it from her mind, it wouldn't be easy. Reporting the incident to Justus' school would be the proper thing to do; however, she'd invested a lot of time in Justus, and to cause another promising black youth to fail when this might have been a momentary lapse in judgment would be detrimental, so she decided to keep it to herself. But apparently, Justus hadn't.

Chapter 3
Social Media the Adversary

It didn't take long for Celeste's accusation of child molestation by Malika to go viral. Not a soul had heard Malika's voice—a cry of innocence. The school system for which she was doing the work for, local law enforcement, and the Department of Social Services had no knowledge of the accusations that had been made against her by Celeste; not until it exploded on social media.

"Unfair" wasn't the word. In Malika's mind, it was blatant disrespect for an innocent person like herself. She had been arrested, tried, and hung by a jury of people who populated the social media platforms of Facebook, Twitter, and Instagram. In less than an hour after Celeste's post about the claim her son had made to her, there were 300,000 hits, with people voicing their undocumented and unsubstantiated opinions without having a clue who Malika Price was.

As the tally grew larger, mainstream radio and television stations jumped on the bandwagon, wanting answers, and begging for the guilty party to speak out. At seven in the evening, a knock at Malika's door gave newsmakers headlines for the next few days. *Good Morning America, CBS This Morning, and the Today Show* were all on top of the story, contributing to the idea of guilt since Malika had yet to say anything. They flashed pictures of Justus and his mother as she ranted on and on about her son being mentored by an old pedophile who needed to be locked up and thrown in prison for the rest of her days.

Malika peered through the peephole. The county's social service worker director and three representatives from the Raleigh City Police Department stood on

Malika's doorstep. Malika exhaled, and then opened the door.

"Yes, may I help you?" Malika asked, although she was aware of why they had come.

Pulling out her credentials, a black woman, somewhere in her mid-forties, dressed in a somber brown shirt-dress, pushed her identification forward for Malika to read. "I'm Mrs. Sherita Carol from the Wake County Social Service office."

"I'm Detective Samosa," the heavy-set dark-skinned man dressed in civilian clothing stated. "And this is Detective Timmons." He pointed to the thin, Caucasian gentleman who accompanied them. "May we come in?"

Malika stared at them, but not wanting any more trouble than what Celeste had already caused, she stood aside and ushered the trio into her house. It was a modest house in the southwest part of town, stylishly decorated with traditional furniture; a neat Bellingham gray sofa, love seat, and chair in the living room. Family pictures, a two-door refrigerator, a white oak wooden table and chairs, and a gas stove were located in the kitchen. A modest dining room set made of mahogany wood filled the dining room space.

"Please sit," Malika said, extending her hand to the furniture in her living room.

The officers and the social worker sat down.

"We've been sent here, Ms. Price, to ask you some questions about one of the students you mentor by the name of Justus Miller," Detective Samosa said. "You are familiar with Justus Miller, aren't you?"

"Yes," Malika answered. "I mentor Justus at least three times a week at my Academy, Teach One, Reach One. I have anywhere from twenty to twenty-five young men of color who come to my academy each year, recommended by their school." Malika took a breath, then continued as the others listened intently, the social worker taking notes. "I've been doing this for years and have never laid a hand inappropriately on any child under my supervision. Whatever Justus told his mother is an outright lie. I'm a good Christian woman. My coworkers and church family can vouch for me if need be."

Mrs. Carol looked up from her notepad she'd been writing on. "Ms. Price, this is a serious allegation."

"I agree, but totally without merit." Malika stood her ground, unshaken by the accusing look the social worker was giving her.

"We are going to have to do an extensive background check on you," Mrs. Carol stated, "which means that you'll not be allowed within fifteen feet of your students or any other children."

"You've got to be kidding me." Malika's voice was controlled, but she wanted to scream to the rafters. "I've done nothing but give my life to this community to the benefit of those students, who I might add have excelled in their studies and have gone on to do remarkable things in this area and around the nation. The last thing on earth I'd do would be to jeopardize all that I've worked hard for—these young black male students."

"Why are you catering only to male students." Mrs. Carol cleared her throat and then eyeballed the two gentlemen. "Excuse me, I mean, *black* male students, as you pointed out?"

Fire lit up Malika's eyes. "Because they are far behind their female counterparts, and when I suggested doing a project to help my community, targeting black male students was suggested. I agreed and accepted the offer to do it under my own umbrella."

"Why, then, would Justus Miller say that you touched

him if you didn't?" Mrs. Carol asked.

"I'll tell you why," Malika said. "He came on to me a few weeks ago. He tried to kiss me. However, I told him no, and what he tried to do was wrong and I wasn't having it. I also told him that he couldn't come back to the academy, but I assured him I wouldn't tell anyone."

Mrs. Carol seemed perplexed. "Why would you tell him that? The first thing you should've done was report it to his school principal."

"Justus was a great student up to that point. If I told on him, all the mentoring that I'd done to see him excel would've been for naught. I was willing to forgo telling on him than to see him become a statistic."

"Ms. Price, you should've used better judgment."

"Mrs. Carol, you're black, as I am, and you of all people should understand where I'm coming from."

Mrs. Carol gave Malika a frothy look. "I've got a job to uphold, and that includes taking predators like yourself off the street."

Malika gritted her teeth. "I did nothing to that boy. The tabloids, news headlines, and social media can say all they want, but no one until this day has approached me to get my side of it. I'm going to hold my head up high because I'm not a predator. Now you may excuse yourself if you don't have anything else to say."

Officer Timmons cleared his throat and then stood. "Ms. Price, we have to ask you to come down to the police station with us. Charges have been filed against you, which means you must come with us. You'll probably be placed under custody until a bail hearing is set. Can't say much more until you've reached that point."

Malika shook her head. She frowned at the three people who sat in her house looking back at her. "There's truth to the saying, 'don't let your good be evil spoken of.'

I've laid down my life to help these children. God bless them."

Chapter 4
Shame the Devil

The insults, the ugly memes, and the vicious language continued to pour from the pages of social media. Some ugly soul even dared to produce a video of baby chicks in the barnyard and the mother hen (with Malika's face plastered over the actual hen's face), running after her baby chicks, shooing them into the hen house for whatever someone's dirty imagination conjured up. Malika had been called everything except a child of God. It wasn't until this incident that she'd become fully aware of how mean and cruel people could be to one another—people she didn't know. Even people as far away as across the pond in England, Germany, and France put in their two cents.

She refused to go to church and didn't attempt to go to the academy that had been ransacked and vandalized by malicious graffiti. It didn't matter where she was being attacked, the media had outed Malika as a child predator, and that she'd used her school to gather her subjects. Her only saving grace was that other boys, some of whom were now young men, and their families stated that Malika was nothing but a blessing and a God-send. Those who were questioned about their experiences being mentored by Malika claimed she was the ultimate teacher, and only had their best interest at heart.

As the media blitz died down, the folks in and around town couldn't get Malika Price's name out of their mouths. People pointed when they went past her house. She'd almost have rather stayed in jail—the few hours she was in there—than submit to the constant threats and humiliation she received either by phone, by some random brick thrown at her house with a note taped on it, or by people walking by her house with signs of protest. The ordeal had broken Malika's spirit down until she felt unworthy and that God had forsaken her. She'd given so much, but in return, she felt like she was close to hell's gate.

Then she heard a voice. It was as clear as a whistle. The voice told her to get up and not be weary. *"I haven't abandoned you. You've got to put on the full armor and fight the devil and his evil forces. I'll be standing right with you, fighting the false allegation, the abuse, the name-calling, and those haters who rode the waves of social media to intimidate, destroy, and blemish a good woman. Rise up, woman of God. Forgiveness isn't always forgetting, but it's a cleansing you need to fight the battle."*

Without another minute passing, Malika rose from her pity party state, showered, and put some comfortable clothes on. As she was going about getting ready, a song by Fred Hammond titled "We're Blessed" came to her that she began to sing. With a renewed sense of spirit, Malika walked out of her house for the first time in two weeks.

Chapter 5
Forgiveness

Shady Grove Baptist Church was behind Malika Price every step of the way. They knew the kind of person she was, especially as a member in good standing for most of her life. They rallied around her and started a GoFundMe page to help pay for her legal expenses. Many of those who'd gone through her program and had prospered under her tutelage were benefactors to her cause. They gave generously, as Malika had done for them.

A civil rights attorney, who was a member of Shady Grove, took up Malika's cause. The trial was set for some time in the following year; however, due to the charges, Malika wasn't allowed to teach. In fact, she thought about closing the academy down for good, especially since the grants that helped subsidize what she was doing were being withdrawn. She'd given up her career as a high-school teacher to do what she couldn't do under the supervision of the school board.

Prior to the trial, there would be meetings of the attorneys involved. There would be discoveries, negotiations, and a settlement if it came to that. It was going to be a hard-fought trial, as there was no actual proof, only he said-she said. The real trial would be in the media, where the fire had been fueled.

Several weeks had passed since Malika had entered the center. With all the notoriety that had come with the accusation, Malika was no longer allowed to mentor any youth. Today, a burning in her heart prompted her to get up and go to the center, even if it was to simply look at the edifice, although the truth of the matter was that her life's work was entrenched in the building; every nook and cranny, including the books and furniture.

Dressed casually, Malika drove the five miles to the center. Upon reaching her destination, she pulled into the parking area, turned off the ignition, and sat staring. Again, all her undertakings—the triumphs, and successes that her love for her students had achieved—came rushing back as she continued to stare. A tear ran down her cheek. While there was a black cloud over the center, Malika silently thanked God for all the charitable deeds that had been rendered, and the wonderful achievements that seemed to make the dark cloud disappear. She was thankful for those persons who continued to support her, while the savages who hated her guts tried to shred her to pieces in the media.

No longer in dread of going back to the center, Malika got out of her car and went inside. She brushed the top of the tables and chairs with her hands as she passed through one of the classrooms in route to her office. She stood and twirled around, remembering the first student she mentored, who had gone on to medical school at John Hopkins. She smiled.

The smell of the place was all-consuming. It was a mixture of wood, sweat, and love. The air was musky, as the place had been closed for several weeks, but a smile rippled across Malika's face as she continued toward her office.

Once in her office, sitting down in her chair, she toyed with a few knickknacks that were on her desk. Taking a brief scan around the room, she nodded her approval that all hadn't been lost. Somewhat in a daze, she sifted through a few papers that sat on her desk, until her fingers stopped at an unopened envelope.

She wasn't sure when it came. Had she placed it on the desk and failed to open it? No one could get into the place but her and her support staff. She hadn't seen her assistant, Lilly, in the past three weeks, though it would explain how the unopened piece of mail got on her desk.

Malika was about to pick up the envelope when she heard a noise. Someone had come into the facility. Her body tensed, but she rose from her seat and inched quietly toward the door to her office. She poked her head out but didn't see anyone.

There was the noise again—a door opening. Tense and nervous, Malika called out. "Who's there?" There wasn't an immediate answer. "Who's there?" Malika called out again.

Silence.

And then there were footsteps so close that she froze where she stood. A head peeked in the door. Malika was suddenly frightened, not knowing why Justus was lurking at the entrance to her office.

Her eyes became round as saucers. Malika stared at him without uttering a word. Her eyes softened. "Justus?"

"Ms. Price?"

"What . . . are you doing here?" Malika stammered, her nerves starting to get the best of her.

"I . . . I wanted to know if you read my letter."

Malika looked down at the envelope on her desk.

"I saw your car in the parking lot. I wanted to talk to you."

Malika looked back up at her former student. "No, I haven't read your letter. I'm not sure that you should be here, Justus, considering all that has been going on." Malika looked at him sternly. "Since I was accused of something I didn't do."

Justus' eyes swept the ground until he found the courage to look back up at Malika again. "That's what the letter is about. I'm sorry, Ms. Price. I didn't mean for this to happen to you. I lied . . . I lied because you hurt my feelings. I thought I was in love with you. I had been fantasizing about you a lot. And that day . . . that day when I tried to kiss you, you took my fantasy and ripped it apart."

Malika tried to compose herself. She knew better than to go over and give Justus a hug for fear of reprisal, especially in light of what she'd already been through. But the compassionate side of her couldn't help but feel sorry for him. Still, she didn't want anything else misconstrued.

"Have you told your mother what you told me?" Malika asked.

Justus shook his head. "Not yet."

"Why not, Justus? I've been brutally demonized in the media. I can no longer help students like yourself. All of that is because I was falsely accused of touching you inappropriately, which you and I both know is a blatant lie."

"I'm sorry, Ms. Price. I'm not sure I can tell my mother what I did."

Another voice came out of nowhere. "I heard everything, Justus." Justus' mother walked through the door, dressed in jeans, an ocean-blue tank top, and flip-flops. "I happened to pass by in my car when I saw you enter the building, and thank goodness I turned around and came in," Celeste said. She threw her hands on her hips. "You've got me looking like a fool, son."

"What did you hear?" Justus asked his mother.

"Almost all of your confession. Your lie that started this all. You owe this woman an apology."

"Mama, I've already told Ms. Price that I was sorry."

"Now, you'll have to go to your school and tell your teacher too."

"None of this would've happened if you hadn't put it out on Facebook. You're the one that needs to apologize."

"Don't sass me, boy!" Celeste said at the top of her lungs. "I'll knock you into next week."

Malika was a little taken aback at Justus's words to his mother, but he'd said what was on Malika's mind. While Justus planted the seed, Celeste was the one who watered and pollinated it throughout all media outlets. Yes, she needed to render an apology as well.

A lone tear slid down Justus' face. "I'm really sorry, Ms. Price. I hope you'll forgive me for what I've done. We need you. You're the best, and I don't want you to pay for my stupidity."

Both amazed and grateful at his apology, Malika smiled and stood in front of Justus. "I'm sure that was hard for you to say, but I appreciate your honesty. Now I can reclaim my good name, and hopefully I'll be able to help others. I forgive you, Justus. It was a hard lesson for the both of us. Now, why don't you go on while I talk with your mother privately."

"Okay. Thanks." Justus turned and walked out of the room, leaving Malika and his mother along in the office.

"That's a smart young man you have," Malika began. "I truly hope that this incident doesn't hurt his future in any way. But I think your son is right," Malika said, "you owe me an apology. You were very ugly to me the morning you came here with that cruel accusation . . . false accusation."

"Look, I'm going to do what I need to do. But what was I supposed to do when my son comes to me telling me that some older woman had put her hands on his privates? Lady, you ought to be glad that I didn't knock you out."

"Well, I'm glad you didn't, however, I've suffered tremendously from all of your actions surrounding this. I told you I didn't do it, but you refused to believe me, and then turned around and put that smut out for the entire world to see." Malika waved her hand. "You know what? I don't need an apology from you. Justus' apology was sufficient. Just know that while I've forgiven, I haven't forgotten."

"Suit yourself, honey." Celeste shrugged her shoulders. "But I will put something out on Facebook."

"That's all I can ask, I suppose. Thank you for stopping by." Malika looked toward her office door, hinting to Celeste that she could now make her exit.

"Okay." Celeste nodded her head and disappeared the way she had come.

Malika sighed and went back to her desk and sat down. Ingesting all that had occurred in the past fifteen minutes, she picked up the envelope that was addressed to her. She stared at her name written in pencil.

Curiosity getting the best of her, Malika flicked the envelope up and down between her fingers, finally setting it down on her desk. Turning it over, she reached for her letter opener, and with one easy stroke, sliced opened the envelope and took out the contents. It was a one-page letter signed by Justus.

Dear Ms. Price,

I'm sorry for all that has happened to you. I didn't mean for it to happen. I lied to my mother about you touching me. I was mad because you didn't kiss me back and made me feel like a little kid. I was wrong and I'm sorry.

I . . . we need you back at the center. I told some of my boys the truth and they're really mad at me. I don't know how to tell my mother the truth because she can be abusive sometimes, and she will go off when I tell her. I wish she hadn't posted that stuff on social media. If you forgive me, maybe we can find a way to get you back. Again, I'm sorry.

Justus Miller

Tears began to form in Malika's eyes. She hadn't expected to receive a heartfelt letter expressing forgiveness from, of all people, Justus. The words touched her heart; her efforts weren't in vain. The paper rattled as Malika's hands began to shake a little. Full of gratefulness, all she could seem to do was bow her head and weep.

Chapter 6
Fix it, Jesus

Tears of joy ran rampant through Shady Grove Baptist Church. Malika had just read aloud the letter she'd received from the school board. She had been exonerated of any wrongdoing and they wanted her to reopen the center as soon as possible. Her grants had been reinstated, and when people heard what had happened, money from all parts of the city started pouring in to help restore all that she'd lost.

Malika was a true servant of the community; her goodwill produced some of the best and brightest stars. But there was one grant that stopped her cold, as it came with a condition. The grantor wanted her to serve not only black male students, but all male students who needed her kind of guidance. There would be money to provide for employing other mentors.

It was the right thing to do. God loves all the little children.

At Shady Grove Baptist Church, they shouted and praised God until sounds resonated from the rafters. This was a testimony that couldn't and wouldn't stay silent. It was like fire shut up in Malika's bones.

"The Invitation"
Nicole Smith

Chapter 1

"Wait . . . is that the doorbell?" I asked.

"Are you expecting anyone?" asked Anthony.

"No," I said. "I distinctly remember telling my friends what my plans were for tonight."

I politely excused myself from the kitchen dining table. I walked through the living room to the front door. Because I was only five feet four, I had to stand on my tippy toes to look through the peephole.

"Oh my God," I said. Without making a sound, I tiptoed past the kitchen to the back door.

"I can't let him in. He is *not* getting in here," I whispered to myself.

As I put my hand on the doorknob, checking to make sure that it was locked, suddenly his face appeared in the window of the door. I could see his facial outline through the chiffon window curtains. He was unbalanced, as if he had been drinking.

"Oh Lord, and he's drunk," I whispered under my breath.

He began pounding on the door. "Open this door now!" the voice on the other side of the door ordered.

Looking more callous than I had ever seen him, he lifted his shirt and I saw the butt of his gun sticking out of his blue jeans.

"Who is at the door?" Anthony called out.

Ignoring Anthony's inquiry, I kept my eyes on the uninvited guest. I watched him pull out the gun, lift it to eye level, and point it directly at me. That's when he shot off his first round, right through the door.

Running away from the door, I was screaming so loud that I did not hear the shot, but the scream did not silence the pain of the shot as a round hit my left arm. I made it back to the living room and fell to the floor, but not before he was able to shoot a second round. That round missed me.

Now out of eyeshot from him, I was able to reach up with my left hand and grab my cell phone and keys from the coffee table. "Anthony! Anthony!" I yelled, but there was no response.

* * *

Six months earlier . . .

"Lori, come on, baby, it's seven-thirty in the morning. Momma has got to get to this bus stop in the next ten minutes, and Ms. Tammy can't wait to see you."

Lori, my only child, was now three years old going on 20. I always ironed and laid out our outfits for the day the night before, so it usually took us no time at all to get ready. But this morning, for some reason Little Miss Lori decided it would be funny for her to take off all her clothes and to redress herself.

"Look, Momma," she said. "I dressed myself."

Not only were her shoes on the wrong feet, but she

had her underwear over top her pants.

"Oh Lawd," I said to myself. "And I only have ten minutes before it's time to head out the door." So, I said a quick prayer, redressed Lori, and headed down the street to the bus stop. I did not have to be at work until nine, but I had to drop Lori off at Ms. Tammy, the babysitter's house, first. We made it to the bus stop just in time to catch the number eighteen bus.

Lori loved paying the bus fare. I could tell it made her feel all grown up. I picked Lori up to allow her to put the money in the slot. After ten minutes, I rang the bell for my stop.

"Time to go bye-bye," I said to Lori. "Ms. Tammy is waiting for us."

Ms. Tammy's house was only two blocks away. Once we arrived, I shared Lori's underwear outfit story with her. Other children had begun arriving and the parents were saying their goodbyes.

"Hey, lil' momma." Tammy smiled at Lori. "You dressed yourself this morning? Look at you," Tammy said, as she twirled Lori around several times. As she let go of Lori's hand, she turned to me. "I will see you this evening."

"Five o'clock as always," I replied.

Tammy looked down at Lori. "Say, 'Bye, Momma.'"

All I got from Lori was a simple wave. Her focus was already on the other children.

On my way back to the bus stop to catch the number four to work, I got a text from Tammy. I'd just left her house. I couldn't imagine what she wanted already. I read the text.

An index card fell out of Lori's bag as I was looking for her sippy cup. I thought you broke up with Keith last year. We need to talk.

Just the mention of that man's name brought back some bad memories. It brought back memories of who I was then, and why I ever allowed someone like that in my life. But the card also was a great reminder of how far I had come, and the great strides I had made in my life. God was changing me in ways that I could have never imagined. I had begun to truly love myself.

I took a moment to send Tammy a text back.

I did break it off. I will explain later.

Chapter 2

I'm sure Tammy would be waiting on razor's edge for me to return that evening and give her the 411. But for now, work had to come first. I was a single mother with a child to support.

In spite of the extra time I spent on dressing Lori this morning due to her wardrobe change, I arrived at work on time. I got to my desk to find a sticky note on my computer screen.

I reached in my purse to get my lotion. While putting on lotion, I read the note. It was a note from my coworker, Jennifer, that read, "Helen, you are cordially invited to my 15th wedding anniversary dinner being held Saturday, December 17th at 7:00 p.m. at Green Celestial Gardens. The attire is formal."

I looked up from my desk to see Jennifer in her cubicle smiling at me. I stood and headed toward her cubicle just as she headed toward mine. We met each other halfway.

"Mark your calendar, girl," Jennifer said with excitement.

"Jennifer," I said, "that is next Saturday. I don't have time to get my hair done, and I definitely don't have anything to wear. I am gonna need to get a rain check." I wasn't sure if I even wanted to go. I thought that taking a rain check would buy me some time until there was actually a next time. But there was an attitude of such confidence and excitement in Jennifer's voice, I continued to entertain her.

"Oh, yes you do have something to wear," Jennifer said, "And I can hook your hair up." She touched my hair, looked down at my feet, and then gave me the onceover. "We wear the same size shoes and the same size in clothes. I have the perfect dress for you, and, girl, it is sexy." She winked and batted her eyes. "Come over tomorrow night and check it out."

It had been a while since I had been out. Being an accountant had me so busy, not to mention running after a rambunctious three-year-old.

I began to think about the dinner and how much fun it could be. It would give me an opportunity to get out and have some good, clean fun and great food. "Okay," I said with a shrug, giving in. "But I will have to stop by and pick Lori up from the sitter's first and bring her with me."

"Oh no, honey," Jennifer said, "you don't have to do all that. You can ride with me from work, and we will stop by Tammy's and pick her up. I can take you home afterward."

"Okay, if you insist, that will work."

"Then it's a date," Jennifer said, dashing back to her cubicle with excitement.

As I approached my desk, a coworker called from out of the production office. "Helen, you have a call on line one."

A call? On line one? For me?

Who in the world was calling me at work? I thought as I sat down at my desk. It couldn't be Tammy; she always called me on my cell. I hesitantly picked up the phone. "Hello, this is Helen. How can I help you?"

"Hey, girl, this is Keith." There was utter silence. I hadn't heard from or talked to Keith in over a year. How did he get this number? Tammy had talked that man up. Geesh!

"Why are you calling me? What do you want?" I asked, sounding irritated. "I'm working."

"Well, I won't keep you long," Keith started. "But I've had some time to think, and I have been thinking about you. First off, I want to apologize for my past behavior. I want the opportunity to show you that I am a good guy. Can we meet and talk about it?"

I pulled the phone away from my ear and looked at it like I was looking at Keith; side eye in full effect. I put the phone back to my ear. "Keith, we have nothing else to talk about. I said all I needed to say when we last met. And based on the chick that I caught you with in *my* bed, your actions made it quite clear what needed to be said, and you said it very well."

"Well, you see, me and that chick, we ain't together anymore and uhh . . ." He began to stammer. "I would love for us to start all over."

He was a day late and a dollar short. I started thinking about how unhealthy the relationship was. I thought about all the red flags that were there that I purposely overlooked, and why I overlooked them; because I thought he would change. I realized the unnecessary pain that came with being with a man like Keith. I did not understand it then, but I understood it very clear now, and it was not a road I was willing to travel again.

"You missed your chance for any of that to ever happen again. For two weeks after that incident, I just kept getting threatening calls from your chick, so I have moved on. I am going to hang up now, but before I do, I just want to thank you."

"You want to thank me? Thank me for what?" His voice was laced with confusion.

"Thank you for coming into my life. You see, it took me seeing all that you had done and said to me for what it was for me to realize how valuable I really am. I am somebody. You taught me that I am worth more than just someone who decided to stay celibate." I paused to take a breath before continuing. "Keith, I am forty years old, and I knew that I had made a conscious decision to never have sex again until I was married. I have now been single and celibate for almost four years. I promised myself that the next time I have sex with a man, there will be a ring on my finger and he will be my husband. I am sorry you could not accept my boundaries, but thank you, because it has strengthened my belief."

"I am worth more than being just a piece of jewelry on your arm to look good for everyone else to see. I watched you lower yourself to be with women because I chose to stay celibate. I watched you and allowed you to demean me so you could go and do 'your thang'. Well, now I'm doing mine; and it's a *God* thang," I said with attitude. "Again, thank you. Because of you, I was able to move on and be at peace with my decision *and* myself. My only goal is to go forward. I can never go backward. I pray that you see who you really are and don't settle for anything less than what God wants for you, just as I did. It leads nowhere. And please, do not call me again. Bye, Keith, and be blessed."

"But I was good to you, girl." Keith wasn't going to let me end the call so easy. "I gave you everything you wanted and then some. How you just gonna dis me like that? You won't even give me the chance to show you that I have changed," he pleaded. "Girl, I never stopped loving you. I don't care what you saw. I don't care what you heard. I need you to see that I am trying to change."

"Keith, you never loved me, because you never loved yourself. You cannot give me something that you do not have the ability to give. I had to accept that. I love you with the love of the Lord, and that is all I can give you."

With tears in my eyes, I hung the phone up before he could pour any more of his nonsense into my ear gates. It had taken everything in me to share my heart. Keith always had a way of bringing tears to my eyes, but this time, they were true tears of joy instead of pain. It felt so good to share my heart with him, knowing he could never break it again.

* * *

The rest of the day went by quickly. It was almost quitting time when I looked up from my computer and saw my boss walking from his office toward me. He poked his head in my cubicle.

"Helen, can I get the November warranty report before you leave?" my boss asked.

"Absolutely, sir," I replied. "I'll print it to your office printer."

He nodded his appreciation and then headed back to his office, which was only a few feet from my cubicle.

I searched the server for the November warranty report. "August, September, October, November," I mumbled as I scrolled. "Here we go!" I found the report, formatted it, and pressed print. "There you go," I called out. "It is coming to your printer now."

"Awesome, thank you," I heard him reply.

With only five more minutes left before clock-out time, I gathered my things to get ready to leave. On her way out, Jennifer stuck her head in my cubicle. "Don't forget about tomorrow night."

"Okay, see ya. Have a good night."

Jennifer seemed more excited about choosing a dress for me than I did. Oh well, perhaps her excitement would eventually rub off on me.

Chapter 3

After work, I did my usual, which was go by Tammy's house to pick up Lori so we could head home. Just as always, by the time I got to the house, Tammy had Lori all packed up and ready to go so that we didn't miss our bus.

"Thank you," I said to Tammy as I opened the door to leave. "See you tomorrow."

"Not so fast, Helen," Tammy said before I could get out the door. "What is going on with you and Keith?"

"Nothing at all." I smiled. For the first time, it felt good to go back to that place; a place that was painful and full of drama, but also a relief that it was over and my life was getting better.

"I wasn't trying to be nosey, but I am your friend and I care about you," Tammy said. "I see the change and the growth in you. But I know what that man did to you. I watched him make a fool of you. I saw how he talked to you like you were dirt."

"No need to worry, Tammy, like I said, there is nothing going on with me and Keith," I said.

"Then what's up with that note I found in Lori's bag?"

The words Tammy had seen on the index card was a prayer request I'd written requesting God assist Keith in changing his ways, and that he and I could talk without arguing. And I also requested help in allowing me to be a better person to him.

"Girl, that was a prayer request I wrote on the bus last month after he . . . well, you know . . . after our break-up." I didn't feel like drudging up, for the second time today, the incident with Keith and that other woman. "I had written it to put in my prayer journal. I must have left it in the bag."

Tammy shot me a doubtful look.

"Although Keith hurt me so bad, God has taken me past my pain and has encouraged me to pray for his soul. I don't want him back, but I do want him saved. I don't hate him. I want him to be free from his pain too." I placed my hand on Tammy's shoulders. "Thank you, Tammy, for being so concerned."

"Oh, girl, you almost had me worried." She exhaled. "I admire you. You have been single and celibate for so long. I pray that God will give you the desires of your heart."

"Thank you. I appreciate your concern, but, girl, we have got to go," I said while looking down at Lori. "I have to get Miss Lori some dinner, a bath, and some sleep, then do it all over again tomorrow."

"I know that's right." Tammy looked over her shoulder at the couple of children that remained in her living room. "Same here."

"Alright then, I'll see ya, girl," I said as Lori and I left Tammy's and headed to the bus stop.

What a day it had been. I was full of gratitude for the women in my life who only wanted the best for me. It felt great to be a part of such an amazing and supportive tribe. Thank you, God!

I arrived home at last. I had developed a habit of taking my shoes off every time I walked in the front door.

Lori ran in her room and put her backpack on her bed. "Mommy, I t'irsty."

"Okay, baby, sounding just like your granddad," I responded while reaching in the cabinet for her cup. I'd been telling her that as of late, she'd been sounding more and more like my father with his Bahamian accent.

Finally, it was Lori's bedtime, which meant it was "me" time. After a hot shower and a steaming cup of green tea, it was time for my time with my Heavenly Father. Then on to my favorite part of the night, curling up with my pillow and getting the best sleep in the world. I say the best sleep because it was free from worry, free from drama, free from pain, and free from children.

Chapter 4

The next morning, I packed Lori's backpack, and remembering that I had promised Jennifer I would ride home with her to look at her gowns and shoes, I packed an extra outfit, some extra snacks, and Lori's nabi tablet. The forecast was calling for flurries in the afternoon, so I made sure to pack her some gloves, a scarf, and some boots.

After picking up Lori from Tammy's house after work, we headed to Jennifer's to choose a dress. When we first arrived, we went straight to the kitchen to get Lori a bite to eat. After eating some leftover spaghetti Jennifer had, Lori started getting restless.

"I'm going to go put her down in my bed," Jennifer offered. "I'll be right back."

As I waited in the kitchen, Jennifer's husband, Brian, entered the kitchen carrying a bowl.

"Hey, Helen," he greeted as he filled the bowl with potato chips. "How are things going?"

"Great," I replied, "and congratulations on your fifteen-year anniversary. I can't believe Jennifer is still dealing with your behind."

We both laughed.

"Naw," he said, "I'm dealing with hers. Thanks for the congrats. I'm so glad you are coming."

"Thanks for the invite," I said.

He looked around. "Where's Jen at?"

"Oh, she went to lay Lori down for a nap."

"Then join me until she's finished." Brian nodded toward the kitchen exit. "I'm just watching the game."

"Don't mind if I do." I followed Brian to their den, where we chatted about their anniversary dinner. Upon entering the den, the television was tuned to a football game, but we proceeded with our conversation. I soon realized Brian was not alone; he had company. I don't know who the man was, but he sure was fine. I could feel him staring at me as soon as I entered the room.

The voice behind that fine face commented, "Brian, I'm feeling a little left out of the conversation. Aren't you going to introduce me?"

I looked at Brian as if I was agreeing with the stranger. The stranger slowly, but respectfully, stood as if waiting to be introduced.

"Oh, my bad," Brian said, as he took a seat. "Anthony, this is Helen, Helen, this Anthony Johnson, my cousin." He looked to his cousin. "Helen and my wife work together."

"It's nice meeting you, Anthony," I said.

It was like he was not just looking *at* me, but looking *through* me as if he could see everything about me and make me feel okay.

He extended his hand toward me. "No, the pleasure is all mine," Anthony greeted. "Has anyone ever shared with you that you look like that girl from that movie. . . umm?" He thought for a moment. She played the wife in *Enemy of the State*, the wife in *Daddy Daycare*, and the wife in Tyler Perry's Christmas movie."

"You talking about Regina King?" Brian asked.

Anthony pointed his finger toward him, confirming the answer was right. "Yeah, yeah, her."

"Well, thank you, Anthony." I blushed. "I'm flattered, because she is gorgeous."

"And so are you," Anthony said, smiling a perfect smile. "I hope this will not be the last time I see you."

Brian interjected. "Well looka here, looka here. I have a great suggestion if you all are up for it." Brian's attention was on me as he spoke. Now, my wife tells me she has invited you to our anniversary dinner this Saturday." Brian reiterated what they'd already talked about. "I just happened to have invited Anthony as well, and since you're both single and I'm assuming neither of you have an escort, how about you both just go together? You have both been officially introduced now."

"Oh, my cousin, you have made probably the best suggestion ever," Anthony said to Brian, then looked to me. "How about it, Helen? It'll be fun. I mean, if you would like. No pressure, just a night out in honor of my cousin and his wife."

I thought about it for a moment. I imagined myself on his arm and enjoying an evening out. The image alone felt great. "Okay," I nodded, "I would like that."

"Great, can I get your number, and I will give you call so we can set up the details?" Anthony suggested.

"Sure." I began to scrounge around for a pen and paper, but Brian jumped up and gave them to me as if he had been waiting for me to just ask. If I hadn't known any better, I would have thought this entire thing had been a set up.

I took the paper and pencil, wrote down my telephone number, and handed it to Anthony. "Here you go. Anthony, it was nice meeting you."

"Again, the pleasure was all mine," he responded with a smile that lit up the room.

"Brian, good seeing you again." I used my thumb to point over my shoulder. "I'm sure Jennifer is waiting for me," I said.

I left Brian and Anthony to get back to their football game and went in the kitchen where Jennifer was, indeed, waiting for me.

"Look at your face all lit up," Jennifer said as I entered the kitchen. "So, I see you have met cousin

Anthony?" she asked knowingly.

"Yes, I have, and he seems to be a sweet person."

"Helen, he is. He will give you the shirt off his back. A wonderful man of God who loves the Lord." Jennifer began talking as if she was trying to pitch him to me. Little did she know, I was already sold.

"Well, guess what? Brian just shared with me that his cousin is going to the anniversary as well and that it might be a great idea if we go as a couple." I tooted my nose up in the air as if I was one-up on Jennifer.

"Sooo?" Jennifer was hanging on to the edge of her seat.

"Sooo . . . we are making plans to go together," I said.

"What?" Jennifer said with excitement. "Oh, Helen, that is such a great idea! You will enjoy being with him. And he ain't no bum, you know," Jennifer added for good measure. "Anthony is a prosecuting attorney and an extremely handsome one."

"Yes, but girl, it has been a long time since I have been out. I'm not sure if I'm ready." Doubt began to set in.

"Well, it's just a dinner. Friendship is a wonderful thing." Jennifer grabbed my hand. "Come on, girl, and try these dresses on. I think I already know the perfect one for you."

I followed Jennifer to her walk-in closet. She had already set aside three dresses she thought I would like. One dress was white with pearls on the neckline. One was navy blue with chiffon sleeves, and then there it was. It was the one. The third one had a black, cute neckline that went all the way around the neck, leaving the upper and lower back exposed. It was laced from the front sides all the way to the lower back, just above my tailbone. Then at the back on the bottom, there was a small one-foot train.

"That's it, that's it!" I said, pointing at dress number three.

"Well go try it on," Jennifer said to me.

I went in the bathroom to try it on. Minutes later I came out wearing it like a glove. Truly, it was the perfect dress for my medium frame build. I loved everything about it.

Jennifer looked at me with her mouth wide opened in awe. "I knew that's the one you would choose. So, are you saying 'yes to the dress?'"

"Yes, yes, this is it." I was convinced, and so was Jennifer.

She allowed me to choose a pair of shoes from her closet and some jewelry.

"What time is it?" I asked. It felt so late. "I better get going."

Lori had been asleep the entire time, and I really did not want to wake her, but I had to go. Jennifer packed up the dress, shoes, and accessories for me while I scooped up Lori. As I was walking out of the bedroom with Lori in my arms, Anthony met me at the door, coming from the direction of the bathroom that was just down the hall.

"I will walk you both to your car," he offered.

"She doesn't have a car," Jennifer interjected. "I am going to drive her home. She doesn't live that far, so tell Brian I'll be right back."

"If it's okay, I would be more than glad to take you home," Anthony offered to me. He put his hands in the air. "I promise, I don't bite. If you don't feel comfortable, Brian can ride along with us."

"Brian can what?" Brian appeared in the hallway. Anthony explained the offer he'd just made.

I looked at Brian. "I would like that. Would you,

Brian?" I asked him. I then looked to Anthony. "It's just that I really don't know you, and, you know . . ." I looked down at my sleeping princess. "I have my child and all, and being alone, and . . ." I just keep babbling on and on until I finally said to myself, *"Just be quiet and walk out the door!"*

Brian agreed to accompany us on the ride home, which was a pleasant one. It felt good to have a conversation where I felt safe. I was glad Anthony suggested Brian come along, because it made me feel so much better.

* * *

We reached my apartment and Anthony walked me and Lori to the front door. He'd relieved me of the dress and bag, holding it in his hands as I opened the front door. He came inside and laid them on the table for me.

"Would you be okay if I were to call you before Saturday?" he asked. "I enjoyed the conversation in the car and would love to continue it."

"Sure." I smiled. "A good time for me is usually any time after seven in the evening, once I've put Lori down for bed."

"Sounds good," he replied. "Have a great night."

"You too," I said as I watched him walk away.

I closed and locked the door behind him. I then leaned my back against the door. "Okay Lord, what just happened? A fine guy who is a man of God?" I was totally attracted to Anthony, and from what I could tell, he was attracted to me. I just hoped I wasn't moving too fast. And more importantly, I hope he wasn't either. I'd learned from my past that everything needed to be in God's time. "Jesus, help me!"

Chapter 5

On Wednesday, my cell phone rang. I didn't recognize the number, so I didn't answer it. Moments later, I received a chiming notification that I had a voice message. I picked up my phone and accessed the message. It was Anthony. I regretted not having taken the call, as my mind started swirling with all kind of thoughts; thoughts such as Anthony thinking that perhaps I didn't want to talk to him.

"Hello, Helen, this is Anthony," he'd stated in the message. "I know my number may not be familiar, and if you are like me, you probably scan your calls." He let out a slight chuckle. "But now that you know my number, if you feel comfortable, would you please give me a call back? Hope to talk to you soon. Bye."

I decided I had better call him back right away. I could not have that fine man thinking I didn't want to be bothered. I called his number, and once Anthony answered after only two rings, we started to talk. I apologized for missing his call, and before I knew it, we were on the phone for at least two hours.

It had been a long time since I'd had such a drama-free conversation with a man I was interested in and who had no ulterior motives and no demeaning words to utter. I felt free to speak. It was such a peaceful conversation. I needed that.

After ending the call with Anthony, I locked his number in my phone right away. If I could help it, I would not be missing any more of his calls.

Saturday could not have come soon enough. Anthony and I had talked on the phone every night, and I couldn't wait to talk to him in person.

Early Saturday morning, the phone rang. This time, I

not only recognized whom the call was from, but by now I'd assigned Anthony a ringtone. We had made plans for him to come by my house around 6:15 to give us time to stop by Tammy's house and drop Lori off.

Anthony arrived right on time. He was such a gentleman. Everything seemed to come so naturally to him. From opening my door, to offering me his arm, to making sure I felt comfortable. He almost took my breath away with his kindness, not to mention the fact that he was *so* fine.

I gave him the once-over as he returned the same gesture. I'd thought he was fine on the night I met him, but tonight, he was simply breathtaking. He was not wearing that black tuxedo—that black tuxedo was wearing him!

His jacket fit him perfectly from the shoulders to the biceps, right down to his wrist, where the cufflinks seemed to match the gold watch on one wrist and the gold chained bracelet on the other. The smell of his cologne—oh my goodness—just made me want to holler! Well, I did holler, using my "inside voice." He heard me and he smiled.

The very first thing he said to me was not with words, but it was with a look. He stared at me for at least five minutes . . . well, it felt like five minutes. Then he said, "You are not just beautiful on the inside, but outside too. It's almost like God's love shines from within you, and He allows others to see it on the outside." He gave me another head-to-toe onceover. "You look amazing. Jennifer hooked you up, hair and everything."

"Wow! Thank you, Anthony." I blushed. "You're looking very dapper yourself tonight."

"Well, I try." He popped his collar while giving himself a modest once-over. He winked at me, and then turned to Lori, bending down to her eye-level. "Look at you, little Miss Lori, with your blue hair bow matching your blue purse."

Lori responded with a shyness that I would expect from someone that she was not familiar with. As she turned to the side, she pressed her face into the side of my dress, hiding from Anthony.

Motioning us to the car, I put Lori in the back seat and Anthony held the car door open for me to get in as we headed to Tammy's house.

After dropping off Lori, the ride was so relaxing. It was natural for Anthony to take our conversation and just continue so smoothly. He was so easy to talk to, and he was quite understanding. He began to share with me his goals in life and how spending time with me was a part of those goals. We talked about his family and how much he missed them. He even began to open up about his last relationship. He was a man of God, and he desired to stay celibate, but it seemed that he could find no one who was on his same path, until now.

"I want to thank you for agreeing to let me escort you," Anthony said. "It's been a minute since I've been out with a young lady." Pulling up to the stop light, he looked in my direction. "I am excited about tonight."

I could see the excitement in his eyes, or at least that's what I assumed the sparkle in them was.

"You are very welcome," I said sincerely. "It has been a while for me too. But you have made it easy for me. Thank you."

Just ahead was the turn into the gardens where the valets were waiting. After pulling up to the front and getting out of the car, Anthony opened the door for me and immediately offered me his arm. Hand-in-hand, we arrived at the front steps. A crystal waterfall met us at the entrance, and a red beaded carpet followed. I held on to

Anthony's arm as tight as I could, enjoying every single step.

I could feel the flow of my train on my black gown as it rested smoothly on the red carpet. I looked back to see if I needed to lift the train of the dress, but the black gown on the red carpet looked so elegant, I felt like a princess shining with her prince. Anthony placed his hand on the small of my back, as if to guide me on the path. I was glad my back was exposed because his touch made me feel secure.

As we arrived inside, there were white bouquets of flowers on each table with a miniature waterfall in the center of the bouquet. Everything was beautiful.

We saw Jennifer in the distance. It was almost as if she was getting married all over again. As Anthony and I walked toward her, and she walked toward us, I couldn't help but notice how stunning she was.

"We have a table for you right here." Jennifer pointed to the front table where she and Brian would be sitting. She had us seated with them up front and center. The chairs were decorated glamorously with gold spindles on the back and baby breath flowers interweaved on the bottom. Each table had six chairs. I was so mesmerized by the waterfall in the center, I could hardly take my eyes off of it.

Jennifer and Brian headed toward the table to take their seats, and Anthony and I followed suit.

Anthony pulled the chair out for me and sat close. Jennifer and Brian played lovey-dovey while Anthony and I held a conversation of our own.

"Anthony, so, I have a question for you," I started. "I love seeing family so close. I notice that you and Brian are very close. I know you two are cousins, but are you first cousins, second cousins . . .?"

"First cousins," Anthony answered. "His mom and my mom are sisters. My mom passed with breast cancer when I was fifteen years old, and my aunt, Brian's mom, raised me. So, he is like a brother." Anthony stared off for a moment, reminiscing. We did everything together, and we were born in the same year. His birthday is in June and mine is in September."

Anthony looked over at Brian, who was so enamored with Jennifer that the two had probably forgotten Anthony and I were at the table with them.

"Yeah, I truly respect him and look up to him," Anthony said. "He is a great example of a good man and always has my back."

"That makes perfect sense." I nodded. "I'm sure it was great to have someone to grow up with and to ease the pain of your mother passing away."

We shared more details about our upbringing and families until a waiter arrived with a tray. We began to eat and the conversation shifted to favorite foods and restaurants. I was glad that no else ever showed up at the table. It gave us an opportunity to spend time with each other as well as Jennifer and Brian.

The dinner they served was great. Once speeches were given and dessert was served, I realized it was nearing the end of the event and it was getting late.

"Okay, Cuz," Anthony said, pushing himself from the table and standing up. "We need to be heading out, but congrats on fifteen years of love, and may you have many, many more." Anthony grabbed the back of my chair and held it as I got up. He offered his hand to assist me. "We have to stop by and pick up Lori and get her and her mom home at a decent hour."

Anthony and I reached out and gave hugs to both Jennifer and Brian. Brian and Jennifer walked us to the front door, and Brian gave Anthony a fist bump.

Chapter 6

After picking Lori up from Tammy's, Anthony walked Lori and me to the front door. He gave me a tight hug and it felt as if he was never going to let me go. I wouldn't have been mad if he hadn't—I could have held on all night. It wasn't ten minutes after I'd closed and locked the door that I heard Anthony's ringtone and saw his name show up on my phone's screen.

"Hello," I answered.

"Hey, Helen," Anthony said. "Just checking to make sure you all are in and all is well."

"Yes, we are. Thank you for calling. Tammy had already fed and bathed Lori. All I had to do was put her to bed."

"So, do you have a minute to talk?"

"I do." I sat down on my bed.

"How do you think tonight went?"

"Great! It was wonderful. I laughed, joked, and I learned a lot about you."

"Oh, did you now? And what did you learn?"

I laid back on my bed like a giddy schoolgirl. "I learned that you have a fun and competitive nature."

"Competitive? What makes you say that?"

"You and Brian are a mess. The whole night, both of you kept ragging on each other. When he said something about you, you made sure you got him back harder, and he did the same thing. It was really just clean fun. I loved it."

"Well, I enjoyed your company as well. I enjoyed it so much, I would love to take you out to dinner this coming Friday. That is, if you are available."

"I would love to. I will ask Tammy tomorrow if she will watch Lori."

"Well, I thought maybe we could give Tammy a

break. Jennifer and Brian have let me know that they would be more than happy to watch Lori for you."

"Oh, okay, that sounds good."

"Okay, so, is it a date?"

"It's a date," I said, smiling from ear to ear.

"Great, because I am looking forward to spending more time with you. I love your personality and your spirit is so real. You make me laugh, and I have not done that in a long time." I sat up in the bed and muffled a yawn. "Well, I will say goodnight and I will talk to you soon."

"Good night, and I'll talk to you soon as well."

I ended the call, then shook my head. "Not soon enough!"

* * *

For the next three months, Anthony and I spent almost every Friday night together. That was our day. We did everything from dinner, picnics, and movies, to go-carting, miniature golfing, and fishing—which was a first for me—to me visiting his church, him visiting mine, to working out together. However, there was one place we had not eaten at together—my house. He had not hung out at my house longer than the few minutes when he'd come inside to pick me up or drop me off. He had not yet even tasted my food. I felt that I was ready and bold enough to invite him to dinner at my home, so this particular week, I suggested that I cook dinner for him. He was elated.

On Friday, I got home early so that I could start dinner. Lori stayed at Tammy's, so I was able to cook free of interruptions. I looked at the clock and it was nearly time for Anthony to arrive. I hurried and changed into the outfit I had bought just for this occasion—a white, off the shoulder blouse that went the length of my thighs and was paired with black leggings.

At 7:00 p.m. on the dot, the doorbell rang, and standing on the other side looking just as handsome as ever was Anthony.

"Welcome to my humble abode," I said, opening the door and swinging my arm up in the air.

Anthony swung his hand from behind his back and handed me a vase with a single red rose in it. "A rose for my rose."

"Thank you. You are so sweet." I accepted the rose and inhaled the wonderful scent.

Anthony stepped inside and began looking around as if he was searching for something. "Wow, something smells great." He inhaled the aroma in the air the way I had inhaled the scent of the rose.

"Good, because it's gonna taste even better."

He followed me from the living room into the kitchen. I walked over to the kitchen sink and placed the rose on the windowsill. Meanwhile, Anthony had made a detour to the stove.

"Oh my," he said as he lifted the lids of the pots. "Pork chops, macaroni and cheese, and broccoli." He looked on the countertop next to the stove. "Is this baked apple pie?"

I laughed, amused by his actions. "Yes, sir."

"Well, let's eat." He rubbed his hands together.

I had the table set for two with two tall center candles already lit. I placed the plates on the chargers. They say the way to a man's heart is through his stomach. I hoped to touch his heart tonight.

We sat down, and he reached across the table to grab my hands and he began to pray. I peeked and opened one eye. I thought to myself, *He's fine, a man of God, and can pray. Jesus, help me!*

Once he finished praying, I scooped up some mac and cheese onto my fork. I paused before eating it. I wanted to watch him take a bite first and see his response.

Wiping his mouth with his napkin, Anthony looked up and then paused. "You really put your foot in this one. Yes, you did." He put his fork down and placed his napkin in his lap. "I have something that has been on my heart that I need to share with you."

Chapter 7

"Wait . . . is that the doorbell?" I asked.

"Are you expecting anyone?" asked Anthony.

"No," I said. "I distinctly remember telling my friends what my plans were for tonight."

I politely excused myself from the kitchen dining table. I walked through the living room to the front door. Because I was only five feet four, I had to stand on my tippy toes to look through the peephole.

"Oh my God," I said. Without making a sound, I tiptoed past the kitchen to the back door.

"I can't let him in. He is *not* getting in here," I whispered to myself.

As I put my hand on the doorknob, checking to make sure that it was locked, suddenly his face appeared in the window of the door. I could see his facial outline through the chiffon window curtains. He was unbalanced, as if he had been drinking.

"Oh Lord, and he's drunk," I whispered under my breath.

He began pounding on the door. "Open this door now!" the voice on the other side of the door ordered.

Looking more callous than I had ever seen him, he lifted his shirt and I saw the butt of his gun sticking out of his blue jeans.

"Who is at the door?" Anthony called out.

Ignoring Anthony's inquiry, I kept my eyes on the uninvited guest. I watched him pull out the gun, lift it to eye level, and pointed it directly at me. That's when he shot off his first round, right through the door.

Running away from the door, I was screaming so loud that I did not hear the shot, but the scream did not silence the pain of the shot as a round hit my left arm. I made it back to the living room and fell to the floor, but not before he was able to shoot a second round. That round missed me.

Now out of eyeshot from him, I was able to reach up with my left hand and I grabbed my cell phone and keys from the coffee table.

"Anthony! Anthony!" I yelled, but there was no response.

I went to call out his name again, but by now, Anthony was already running toward the living room.

"What the . . .?" Anthony said. "Was that gunshots?"

I nodded, out of breath. "It's Keith," I panted out in a hushed tone. "He's at the back door with a gun. He shot me in the arm and he looks like he has been drinking. He's out of his mind!"

"Oh my God, baby, you are bleeding?" Anthony ran to where his jacket was and searched vigorously through his jacket pockets. "Where is my cell phone?" he mumbled. Looking away from his jacket from time to time, he said, "Stay still, baby, stay still."

I began crawling to the hall closet just when I saw Anthony retrieve his cell phone.

"Operator," he said into his phone as he made his way over to me, "two rounds have been fired in the house from outside, and my girlfriend has been shot." He paused for a moment as he looked at me with worry in his eyes. "Yes, I believe he's still here on the premises." Just then, there was a loud thump at the back door. "He's at the back door trying to get in."

Having opened the closet door and seeing my struggle to retrieve a towel, Anthony grabbed one for me. While still on the phone with the operator, he wrapped it around my arm. "Apply pressure. I'll be right back. The operator said officers were in the area and should be pulling up."

That was a relief to hear. As Anthony went to leave, there was a knock at the door. Anthony investigated before opening by looking out the peephole.

"Police, open up!" I heard someone call out.

Anthony let out a huge gust of wind and then opened the door.

Two officers stood at the door.

"Good evening, sir, "I am Officer Jones and this is my partner Officer Cook." He nodded toward his partner. "We received a call that shots have been fired and that someone has been hurt."

"Yes, come in," Anthony said, then started walking in my direction. "It's my girlfriend. She's been shot in the arm. I think she was just grazed."

Officer Jones looked at me as he pulled out a walkie-talkie and called for backup. "Stay right here." He held his hand out to me and Anthony. Where is the shooter now?"

Officer Cook began communicating on his own walkie-talkie. "The shooter is still armed and at the back door," he reported upon concluding his conversation.

Officer Jones proceeded in the direction of the back door with his gun drawn, peering behind the wall first, looking toward the kitchen, making sure it was clear. Without even going in the kitchen, I could tell by his actions he could see Keith. He dipped back in and cocked his weapon.

His partner immediately went to his side.

With pistols drawn, the two officers disappeared out of our site, headed to the back door.

"Don't move! Police!" we heard one of the officers shout. Next, we heard scuffling and more yelling.

By this time, curiosity had gotten the best of us. Anthony and I crept closer to the back door.

"Suspects down," one of the officers said.

I looked at Anthony, confused. "What?" I asked. "*Suspects?*"

Come to find not only had Keith shown up on my doorstep shooting, but Charlie, Tyrell, and Clyde—three of his friends—were also with him. I don't know if they were trying to stop the fool, or if they were all cut from the same cloth and had shown up to damage as well.

I looked at Anthony and did not—could not—say a word. All I could do was make a simple gesture; a gesture that looked as if I wanted to ask a question. Anthony gave me a reassuring look as if to say, "Everything is going to be okay."

When Anthony and I heard the sirens of an ambulance, we headed toward the front door. As we made our way back to the living room, Anthony said, "You're still bleeding. Stay right here."

He went to the linen closet and grabbed another towel. He took the bloody towel off my arm and gently wrapped the clean towel around my wound. "There you go," he said as he reached his arms down toward me. "Now put your other arm around my neck and hold on tight. Keep plenty of pressure on that arm."

He picked me up and carried me in his arms, headed for the front door.

"Can you get my purse, keys, and my cell phone, please?" I asked him. "They are all right there on the table next to the couch." I nodded in the direction of the couch and winced. The pain in my arm was throbbing. Applying pressure was painful, but I knew I did not want to lose any more blood.

He picked up my purse and put the keys and phone inside of it while I held on tightly to him so that I wouldn't fall from his arms. He then gently placed the purse onto my stomach. With me still in his arms, he opened the front door and met the EMTs that were coming toward the house with a stretcher in tow. He placed me carefully down on the stretcher.

"Can you lock up for me?" I asked Anthony, who did just that.

The EMTs secured me and then transported me to the ambulance.

"I am right here, I am right here," Anthony said as we arrived at the back of the ambulance. "Looks like you were just grazed. Thank God things weren't any worse."

I nodded, still in a state of confusion, but blessed that, like Anthony said, things weren't worse.

"Sorry about dinner," I said regretfully.

Anthony let out a little chuckle. "Don't worry about that right now, baby. We'll have another chance soon. But you don't get away that easy," he said. "This little incident doesn't scare me. I don't run away that easy. I just thank God for watching over us and allowing the police to arrive so quickly. Now more than ever I know I'm supposed to be exactly where I'm meant to be, so I ain't going nowhere."

Anthony was right. I can only imagine what might have happened had he not been there.

Chapter 8

Inside the ambulance, there were two attendants. One of the attendants took the bloody towel off my arm and replaced it with a huge gauze-looking bandage that extended from my shoulder to my elbow. "You're going to be just fine," he assured me. "You were just grazed."

The other attendant went around to the front driver seat and started the ambulance, ready to pull off.

About that time, both officers came around from the back of the house with Charlie, Tyrell, Clyde, and Keith, all in handcuffs and staggering to the patrol cars. Anthony looked in the direction of the officers as all four were put in two different patrol cars. Again, he said nothing. But the expression on his face said, "You had better be glad the cops got you before I did."

I had never seen Anthony respond this way before. He went into caregiver mode and he did it without hesitation. The look in his eyes said it all, so much so that I shudder to think what he would have done if the police had not gotten there when they did.

Anthony rode with me in the back of the ambulance. A feeling of security permeated through me as Anthony sat beside me holding my hand. For the first time, I felt the genuine protection he offered, and it felt good.

"What was it that was on your heart that you needed to share with me?" I asked, remembering our conversation that was taking place before Keith and his posse showed up.

"There is a little too much going on tonight to compete with that conversation," Anthony said. "Give me another opportunity to have dinner with you and I promise to share it with you then. Okay?" Anthony looked at me, waiting for an answer.

So glad that he wanted to see me again, I could feel a tear welling up, "You want a date and time now?" I said.

Anthony laughed. "Umm, I think it can wait until you get well. So, you had better get well soon, because, I can't wait to share it with you. I have to get it out, and I'm not sure how much longer I can wait. It's like fire shut up in my bones."

The anticipation and curiosity of what Anthony had to tell me kept my mind off my arm.

The ambulance began to pull out of the driveway. I laid my head back and rested, still wondering what Anthony could possibly want to share with me.

* * *

I must have dozed off, because when I woke up, there was Anthony on the side of the gurney going down the hall of the hospital. I could feel myself going in and out. I arrived in a room at emergency room. They moved me from the gurney to the bed. They must have given me something for the pain, but I did not remember a shot or anything. I didn't even recall arriving at the hospital. But I was feeling so woozy that I know they must have given me something.

The nurse removed my bandages and cleaned my wound. I could hear the nurse speaking to me, but I did not respond. I was so out of it.

I heard the nurse say, "Non-emergency." Shortly thereafter, she took my vitals and left the room.

I closed my eyes again and then opened them slowly. Anthony was intently looking around at all the equipment and machines. Then he looked up toward heaven. He closed his eyes and did not say a word. I closed my eyes and took a deep breath. When I opened my eyes, Anthony's eyes were still closed and I saw a tear streaming down his face.

I dozed out of it again for a minute. When I opened my eyes again, Anthony was standing next to me holding my hand. He was praying softly.

"Father, thank you so much for watching over your daughter and keeping her safe. Now give her the strength that she needs to recover and heal," Anthony prayed. "Touch her spirit that she may continue to be used of You. And father, show me what you want me to do. What is it that you want me to learn from this incident? I know you brought her in my life and I am so grateful, but I need your direction on this one. I will forever love you. Amen."

Anthony looked down at me and smiled. He looked up toward heaven again and said, "Thank you, Father." Anthony began rubbing my hair back. "Girl, you gave us a scare for a minute, so glad you're awake."

"What do you mean 'a scare?' What happened?" I asked.

"You went out on us. You're just now waking up."

"Oh my, I thought they might have given me a sedative or something," I said.

"No, Helen, they gave you nothing. You'd lost more blood than we thought and . . ." He paused, as if he didn't want to think the worst. He didn't finish what he was about to say. He simply bent down and kissed my forehead.

"What was that for?" I asked.

"You know, God has a way of allowing things to happen in our lives to sometimes get our attention," Anthony said. "To wake us up, and to remind us of the important things in life. Sometimes we can be so focused on ourselves that we forget our purpose. I think there are times when He wants us to remember why we are here. We tend to forget about Him and who He is. We forget all that He has done for us. We remember the things like our jobs, our children, and bills needing to be paid. Sometimes He just wants to steer us back to our purpose. Sometimes He just wants us to remember how much He loves us. He wants us to remember that His love is an example of how we ought to love one another. He has proven that to us tonight. He has shown us His love in ways that we cannot count."

Another tear slid from Anthony's eye and then there was a long pause. He took a deep swallow. "While you were sleep, I had some time to think. This incident tonight has changed my way of thinking about God, life, and love.

"Helen, I love you. I not only love you, but I am so *in* love with you. I experienced tonight a love that I cannot fully explain. I prayed for you tonight in a way that I have never prayed for anyone else. You have changed me. You make me a better person. I not only love being around you, but I love being in your presence. I love your personality and most of all, your spirit."

Anthony took a deep breath and then continued. "I was going to wait to tell you this, but I have no doubt that God is saying, 'Now.'"

I slowly sat up in the hospital bed with anticipation. I could tell Anthony was about to share with me whatever it was he'd wanted to share with me at dinner. My heart was pounding. The words he'd already spoken alone had me excited. I knew how I felt about him, but he had never expressed his feelings in this way.

"I know I am not perfect," Anthony said. "I have some flaws and some issues that God has been helping me to work out. I am not a millionaire, but I am a great provider. I don't live in a mansion, but God has blessed me with a warm home. I don't drive a Bentley, but what I have will get you where you need to go. I am a hard worker and I love God, and I have fallen in love with you. I will live every day of my life to make you happy. So, with that being said . . ." His words trailed off as he cleared his throat. "Will you make me the happiest man in the world and let me be your husband? Will you marry me?"

Tears of joy are real, as they streamed out of both Anthony's and my eyes like a river. We must have looked like two crybabies. I reached up for him and he held me oh so tight. He pulled back and looked me in the eyes. "Well?"

"Well, yes!" I exclaimed. "Absolutely, I will marry you. I will! I will!"

We embraced one more time. Anthony pulled away, stared at me, then rubbed my cheek with the back of his hand.

"I will always have your back," he promised. "Know that I will."

I nodded. If I didn't know anything else in that moment, I knew that much.

I looked back over the last few months with Anthony, and I saw God's hand with us, and I still saw it in that moment. And to think, it all started with the invitation to Jennifer and Brian's 15th wedding anniversary dinner, an introduction to an awesome man of God.

I looked toward heaven and said within myself, *Thank you, Father, I am so glad I waited. You have given me four years of singleness and four years of celibacy and it was so worth the wait.*

"Touched by Love"
Florence Levy

Footsteps approaching the shadow of a figure unaware;
Life's long journey about to unfold.
The course unknown.

Beside the still waters is where it all began.
Swift gentle cool breezes tingle the spine. The fresh aroma
of fragrances so sweet linger in the air.
Oh, what a delight to meet you there.

The voice calling you by name boldly claims you are mine.
Seeking and searching for long, lost dreams. Plans for your
future you will see.
Indeed, love that has been shown will now be known.

Flashes of sorrow and pain.
Joy and happiness are there, also.
Wishes and longings in your heart
hoping to be discovered one day.

Troubled childhood to reminisce, young adult to frown
upon too.
Finally, a woman has become an aspired model of His love
and grace.
Silver hair has sprung with glamour and style.
Your wisdom is God's gift to you for your trials and
tribulations,

defined by the fire and scars of days gone as reminders.
Enemies were made your footstools,
Yet you showed kindness abundantly.
He knew from the beginning that the end would be filled
with the peace of still waters and bright sunshine.

Now you see the plans I had for you
to grow to be you today.
Yesterday was already planned.
Tomorrow will never be the same.
Your steps are already ordered.
Step out and live and be merry.
You were born to do great things.
Silver and gold will enhance your days forever.
Take my hand and let me guide
you further, my beloved.

Oh, how great it is to be touched by His amazing grace.

About the Authors

Florence Levy is enjoying retirement. She is elated to be able to spend time relaxing as well as reading novels and poems. Her favorite books are inspirational stories that while reading, make her feel as if she is experiencing what the author is writing. It is that passion that has inspired her to write poems and stories that others can relate to or enhance their lives. Her quiet time has led her to write poetry, including "Silent Tears," "You Don't Know Me," and "Touched by Love."

Florence feels that our journey begins the day we are born, and continues through different seasons of our lives. Her hope is the readers of her poems will feel the emotion of love, and sometimes pain, that comes from life's ups and downs, but also experience God's presence and grace. Florence's plan for the future is to continue writing heartfelt, inspirational poems and stories.

Born and raised in Sumter, South Carolina, Florence lives with her husband, Isaac, where after retiring from the military and civil service, they made Fayetteville, North Carolina their home.

You can learn more about the author by visiting her Facebook page at Florence Levy or emailing her at ilevy1@nc.rr.com.

Darlene B. Fair is a retired federal worker with the Department of Defense, and has been a writer of short stories for five years. Her writing career began when Darlene felt the touch of God as He whispered into her soul to write, igniting Darlene's impulse for writing.

Darlene's greatest passion is to unfasten the window of opportunity to express little pieces of her life in stories that capture readers' imagination, life experiences, adventures, heartaches, emotions, and much more.

As the recipient of the Mid-Carolina Senior Games Silver Arts Short Story Contest, Darlene is an award-winning author. In addition to writing, she enjoys creating BeckeyWorks personalized designs for her business.

You can learn more about the author by visiting her Facebook Page at Beckey Fair or emailing her at beckey51@hotmail.com.

Doris Willis Harvin grew up in South Carolina during the 1970's, a time, unlike today's society, when ladies married at a much younger age. Her story, "Tying the Knot," speaks to the experiences of such a young lady.

Doris retired as a paraprofessional from the public-school system, where she developed a passion for helping young people fall in love with reading. She has enjoyed reading many stories to the students over the years. She is working on a series of children's books that she hopes will educate, entertain, and take readers on many exciting adventures.

Doris lives with her husband in Fayetteville, North Carolina. You can reach out to the author by visiting her Facebook page at: <u>Doris Harvin</u> or emailing her at <u>dwharvin@nc.rr.com</u>

Dr. Norma McLauchlin, Journaling Coach, is the author of various writings, books, and journals. She inspires women to embrace spiritual change and live more fulfilling lives. Speaking from the heart of her own experiences as author, wife, mother, co-pastor, instructor, teacher, and administrator, she has the unique ability to connect to women from all walks of life.

Dr. McLauchlin has accepted the call to help women develop their self-esteem and self-worth. Her humility for God's Word and His people is beyond reproach. As she organizes, guides, coordinates, and executes behind the scenes, one could categorize her as a profound minister, teacher, visionary, exhorter, and leader. Her spirit embraces the experiences, gifts, and talents in her local church as well as surrounding communities that leave a breathtaking message of faithfulness, dedication, and commitment to the Kingdom of God.

You can learn more about the author by visiting her at chosenpen.com, freetochoose.info, or by emailing her firstladynorma@chosepen.com.

Follow Norma on Social Media:

Facebook: @chosenpublishing
Twitter: @NormaMcLauchlin
Instagram: #normamclauchlin
YouTube: Freetochoose
LinkedIn: Norma McLauchlin
G Suite: Norma McLauchlin

Pinterest: McLauchlin Norma

Suzetta Perkins is the author of thirteen published fiction novels and one pre-teen book she co-wrote with her granddaughter, Samayya. She's also a contributing author of *My Soul to His Spirit,* an anthology that received the 2006 Fresh Voices Award and was featured in *Ebony* magazine in 2005. Suzetta is the President of the Sistahs Book Club, and is secretary of the University at Fayetteville State University (FSU), her alma mater. She's also on the Board of Directors for the FSU Friends of the Library.

You can learn more about the author by visiting her website at www.suzettaperkins.com or emailing her at nubianqe2@aol.com.

Nicole Smith was born in Albany, New York and moved to Fayetteville, North Carolina, where she was raised. She joined the military and served in the Army National Guard in Nashville, Tennessee for nine years, making her home in Nashville for 28 years. She now resides in Fayetteville, NC. She is a single mother of four adult children, Marquita, Maurice, Desmond, and Destiny.

Nicole is the daughter of the late Pastor Elzabad Ferguson and her mother, Parthenia Ferguson, who now lives with her. She is the 10th of 12 siblings and serves as a minister at New Life Bible Church, where she presides over the Singles Ministry. She is the author of seven *28-Day Devotions for Singles*, five of which are published, and two more to be published in 2019. Book one is *Opened Palms: On Waiting on God*, book two is *Dear Abba Father: Prayer*, and book three is *Passion Fruit: Passions and Desires*.

Nicole writes on subjects that help and encourage singles in their walk with God. Her oldest daughter, Marquita, is her editor and the founder and owner of Vegas Communications. Her oldest son, Maurice, is her illustrator and the founder and owner of Jester Arts.

Outside of singles, she ministers to women's ministries, conferences, retreats, and any capacity the Lord leads her as a minister. Nicole has been invited to speak at many churches, women's conferences, and single's conferences. In her spare time, she enjoys sewing, writing skits, and the spoken word.

You can learn more about the author by visiting her

website at www.openedpalms.com or emailing her at
nicolesmith@openedpalms.com.

Free to Choose Literary Works
Free to Choose Series
Free to Choose Spiritual Growth Studies and Journals

Free to Choose Worthiness...Fall 2013
Free to Choose Journal...Fall 2013
Free to Choose Christ...Fall 2018
Free to Choose to Write...Fall 2018
Free to Choose to Answer His Call...Winter 2018
Free to Choose I've Got to Write!...Winter 2018
Free to Choose Meditation CD...Winter 2018
Free to Choose Forgiveness...Spring 2019
Free to Choose Self-Love...Spring 2019
Free to Choose Love for One Another...Fall 2019
Free to Choose God's Love...Winter 2019
Free to Choose Quiet Time with God...Summer 2019

Chosen Pen Anthology Series

I've Got to Write!
It's Like Fire Shut Up in My Bones...Winter 2018

Free to Choose Freedom Series...Winter 2019

Ministers' Mates Matte...Spring 2020

Christian Fiction Series
"The Hats of First Lady Norma"...Fall 2020